WHEN DARKNESS SINGS

Redemption's Melody

A Novel

DONNA McELROY

QuillandHeartPublishing.com

Editor: Brae Wyckoff
Cover art by GetCovers
Cover assistance by Mark McElroy

Endorsements

Donna McElroy has a heart of gold, a passion for people, and a knack for writing riveting stories! Get ready to enjoy a real page-turner!

- Shannon Ethridge, M.A.
Life/Relationship Coach & author of 22 books, including the million-copy best-selling Every Woman's Battle series

When Darkness Sings—Redemption's Melody is a powerful, intimate portrayal of a young woman's search for peace and significance amidst the turbulent chaos of family secrets, abuse, and personal consequences. This gripping story is written with sensitivity and grace and will leave the reader with a hopeful outlook for the future.

-Dr. Cindy Holman,
Prophetic Director, Kingdom Creativity International

Donna McElroy takes her readers on a cautious journey that makes one hungry for a satisfying outcome. She doesn't disappoint — but not before a few startling twists and turns you can't see coming. Put this piece of artistic writing in the hands of any person holding hope beyond a complicated life! As a professional counselor, it challenged me personally and professionally on how I approach unresolved conflict for myself and others. Looking for more good reads from this exceptional author who stays the course to reveal the possible from the impossible!

-Lisa A. Northway, M.Div.,
M.A.-Marriage and Counseling, Psychology

When Darkness Sings—Redemption's Melody reminds me of the women I have served over the years who are survivors of human trafficking. Women whose lives have been laden with abuse, exploitation, and trauma. They have been broken, no longer seeing their God-given identity. What you will read through the pages of this book is a familiar story of the actual effects of trauma and the road many women can find themselves on, one of destruction, chaos, and fear. Maybe this is a part of your story. Cecilia's story is the story of women around the world. But while Cecilia's life starts in pain and heartache, it ends in being set free by the only One who can truly bring beauty from ashes. I know this story and these characters can help bring light into the darkness of people's hearts. I pray this book brings light into your heart. This is a powerful story of healing and restoration that can profoundly impact everyone who reads it. I pray heaven and earth collide as you follow Cecilia along her journey from brokenness to redemption.

-Andrea McHenry-Former Executive Director of Freedom and Restoration for Everyone Enslaved

In her first novel, Donna McElroy crafts a thoughtful and inspirational narrative around highly sensitive subjects. In a harrowing and emotional journey, Cecilia shows us that there is healing and wholeness on the other side of tragedy and loss. *When Darkness Sings* is more than an engaging read; it's an invitation for the reader to experience *Redemption's Melody* in their own lives.

- Jill Elizabeth Wyckoff
Author & Co-founder, Kingdom Creativity International

When Darkness Sings—Redemption's Melody by Donna McElroy is a profoundly moving and transformative read.

This powerful story brought me to tears multiple times. I found myself deeply connected to the main character's journey through art therapy, which I've recently incorporated into my healing process.

McElroy's masterful storytelling took me on an emotional rollercoaster, culminating in a sense of hope and inspiration that lingers long after the final page.

This book is not just about the pain and struggles of life; it's about the incredible power of forgiveness and the healing that comes with it. It has inspired me to use my own gifts and talents to guide others to Christ and to embrace the redemptive melody that can emerge from even the darkest moments.

Words cannot fully capture the profound impact of this book. It's a testament to the resilience of the human spirit and the boundless grace that can be found in Jesus Christ, our Lord and SAVIOR. I wholeheartedly encourage everyone to read *When Darkness Sings—Redemption's Melody.*

-**Yuri Huntington, M.A. in Human Service Counseling with Specialization in Life Coaching, B.A. Psychology, Author, Podcast Host, Certified Life Coach, and Licensed Brain Health Trainer through Dr. Daniel Amen**

Dedication

This book is dedicated to
those who have been wounded, misunderstood,
and chained to their past mistakes or trauma.
For those who feel there is no way to wholeness,
this is for you.

Acknowledgments

To God, who spoke to my heart in a little cabin in the woods of Oklahoma, *To Write It, To Right It.* Thank You for being with me along this journey. I could never or would never have done this without You. I pray it will touch the hearts of those who find this story in their hands and that my obedience to write this will bless You.

To my husband, Mark. Thank you hardly seems sufficient to express my love and gratitude for how you have helped me. You ensured I had the tools to write with and kept me technically moving forward. You sat by the light of a lantern as I wrote in the dark by the lake. You took me to rivers and mountaintops where I could be inspired to keep writing; your presence was always a source of inspiration. You encouraged me to keep going when I grew weary. Most of all, thank you for believing in me and praying daily. You are a treasure.

To my children, Emily, Alan, and Seth, and my sisters, Emily and Belinda, your love and encouragement have inspired me. I am grateful for your understanding and support during this writing process. It has meant the world to me.

To my friend Becky, whom I have done life with for many years, I will never forget your response after I read the first few written pages to you: "Hurry up and write some more. I need to know what happened to Cecilia." You have listened to chapters all along the way and always encouraged me to keep going. Thank you for making the trip to Austin with me. It was fun visiting Cecilia's alma mater. You are the *one* I could have genuinely dedicated this book to, yet I know you would want it dedicated to many more.

To Shannon Ethridge, you took me into your world of B.L.A.S.T. (Building Leaders, Authors, Speakers, and Teachers) and mentored me to write years before I knew what I was writing. You watered the seed

God had planted in my heart long ago to become a writer for Him. As the seed grew, you pulled the weeds, added fertilizer, and pruned me as needed. Your encouragement and help with critiques always came at just the right times. Thank you for introducing me to my B.L.A.S.T. family.

To my B.L.A.S.T. tribe, Sharon and Tamara. Thank you for the last few years of standing with me and sowing into this book with your prayers, thoughts, laughter, and tears. We need community, and I am thankful for ours.

To Brae, my editor, friend, and founder of Kingdom Writers Association. I first met you and Jill in a cabin in Hallsville, Texas, one rainy afternoon. I thought I was attending a writer's meeting, but it was much more. You showed me the Father's heart of love and taught me the meaning of becoming a scribe for Him. Several years later, you entrusted me to become a leader of scribes in my hometown. You tenderly encouraged me to write and rewrite and helped me cross the finish line to publication. Thank you from the bottom of my heart for your help and for believing in me.

To Amy, thank you for attending our local Kingdom Writers group and becoming my friend and fellow scribe. Your help has been invaluable. You were the midwife who called me to push the baby out. I will always be grateful for our trip to the Outer Banks of North Carolina, where you timed the contractions while I rewrote the book's ending. I can never thank you enough for your prayers, encouragement, and help with all the finalities. You are a fantastic coach, line editor, and author.

To all the beta readers who took the time to read my first rough draft and lovingly gave me feedback: thank you, Sandy, Mae, Bethany, Sharon, Mackenzie, Susanne, Becky, Jill, Mark, and Cindy. Your feedback was so valuable.

To all the prayer warriors who have bathed and birthed this book in prayer—you know who you are. Thank you. I will never forget you.

Pastor Markus Davidson, thank you for your words of wisdom, encouragement, and prayers for me to be faithful to what God put in my heart. Thank you for mentoring me along my journey of freedom in Christ. You and all Rock Hill Christian Fellowship members in White Oak, Texas, have a special place in my heart.

A special thank you to Pastor Mike, Pastor Tim, and the prayer team at Community Evangelical Church in Sinking Springs, PA, for all of your prayers and support. God bless each of you.

To my KWA Ready Writers of PA, thank you for being a part of our local scribal community. You have become like family as we have shared our stories of defeat and triumph, encouraging one another never to give up but to keep writing and rewriting for Him.

Finally, to all the women who have shared their stories of heartbreak and trauma and allowed me to be a part of their healing process. Thank you for trusting me.

ᴘᴀʀᴄʜᴇᴅ ʙʏ ᴛʜᴇ heat, Cecilia pounded the soil in a panic as if expecting a gush of water to erupt at any moment. The sun burned her face as fiery tears merged with salty sweat. Her biceps quivered as her knuckles turned white against the shovel's wooden handle. Blood dripped from her calloused hands, yet she continued to hack at the earth. A gut-wrenching cry sent her to her knees. Flinging the shovel, Cecilia clutched her chest tightly, trying to contain her shattered heart. As she lay in a fetal position, groaning; echoes of the preacher's voice calling sinners to come forward and repent, haunted her.

A thick blanket of ominous clouds engulfed the sun. Spent and limp, she rolled onto her back. Raindrops began pelting her face, washing away the dirt and sweat. The pain in her heart paled in comparison to the churning in her gut. Suddenly, vomit spewed from her mouth as she spiraled into darkness and gasped for air. *Do You even care, God?*

Cecilia lay paralyzed, wondering if she had died and was trapped in a sea of nothingness. She attempted to scream, but deafening silence was all that came from her open mouth.

The familiar voice bombarded her mind…

You'll never be good enough. Nobody is ever going to want you!

Cᴇᴄɪʟɪᴀ ᴅʀɪꜰᴛᴇᴅ ɪɴ and out of consciousness to the sound of sirens.

Mama! Where are you, Mama?

Shhh. Hush now. Amanda's here to pick you up. Hurry out the back door before she knocks, and get home as soon as your class is over!

But Mama, my hand's bleeding.

Here, put this band-aid over it and go on now. Mama grabbed Cecilia's jaw with one hand to pull her close. Don't you say anything, do you hear me?

Band-aid on, Cecilia quietly closed the door. Truth buried. Emotions stuffed. Smile pasted on.

Cᴇᴄɪʟɪᴀ ꜱQᴜɪɴᴛᴇᴅ ᴡʜᴇɴ she felt a nudge on her shoulder and someone calling her name.

"Cecilia, can you hear me? Wake up," the nurse said while reaching for her hand. The warmth of her touch remedied the chill she felt, at least for the moment.

Startled and dazed, she tried to sit up, but a crescendo of resistance brought her back down, pinning her shoulders.

"Hold on, young lady!" said the middle-aged woman wearing a stethoscope around her neck.

"Where am I?"

"You're in the hospital. I'm Lucy, your nurse. Let me help you sit up."

Cecilia quickly looked toward the window to prevent making eye contact and then slumped back down on her pillow.

"How are you feeling this morning? Are you in any pain?"

"No. How did I get here?"

"Your guardian found you unconscious in your backyard yesterday and called an ambulance. Good man. He came with you and sat by your bed all night. One of the nurses told me they heard him crying and whispering things to you. He left around three this morning. Mentioned your brother Joshua would be coming to pick you up today after you're released. Not sure how he knew you would be released today, but he was right."

Guardian? Confused, she remained silent and shook her head, pretending to understand. Her attention shifted to the window sill, where a plant with crimson blossoms laced with velvety leaves shimmered in the early morning light.

"Beautiful, isn't it?" Lucy asked. "He returned this morning before shift change, dropped it off, and said to tell you to plant it in your garden. *You* have a garden?"

"No...just holes."

Lucy rambled on about her garden. Cecilia closed her eyes and Lucy's voice faded.

CECILIA JOINED HER friends at a party the night she first met *him.* Their eyes lingered on one another before he crossed the room with a beer in one hand and a joint in the other.

"Hey, I'm Sean. Do I know you?" he asked. Eyes, dark and cunning, pierced her soul.

"I d-d-don't think so."

"What's your name?"

"Cecilia."

"Do you go to school here?"

"Yeah, I'm a junior at First Flight High School, but after I graduate, I'll attend the University of Texas in Austin."

"Wow! That's a long way from the Outer Banks of North Carolina."

"Exactly."

"I graduated from Manteo High School last year. I'm renting this place and sticking around until I decide what I wanna do. Right now, I do alright taking tourists out on fishing trips," he said, grinning big and handing her the joint.

Inhaling deeply, the binding knots in her stomach unraveled like a docked sailboat being freed. She felt herself being blown in his direction. With every exhale, he pulled her closer. The quivering in her neck and shoulder muscles subsided.

His eyes were filled with desire as he grasped her hand and said, "Let's go."

She had no memory of their causal conversation as they walked across the street and down the beach. She, desperate to be touched and held, him, eager to sow his seed. Under the black sky, with a few stars acting as night lights, ocean waves pounded the shoreline as they both got what they wanted.

Drifting asleep in his arms, she felt him trying to escape her embrace.

"Hey, do you hear that? Someone's calling my name," he said.

"No."

"Wait, there it is again. Listen, someone's calling my name."

The clouds had passed by the moon, leaving enough light for Cecilia to see a woman coming their way.

"Oh, crap! That's my girlfriend." He jumped up and pulled his jeans and t-shirt on. "I gotta go before she sees us. She wasn't supposed to be back until Sunday. Hey, you'll be alright. Give me time to get her far enough away so she doesn't see you. Sorry about this."

"Are you freakin' kidding me?"

"Gotta go," he said as he took off running down the beach. He grabbed the woman's hand and turned her in the opposite direction, never looking back. Cecilia watched as the two of them faded into the blackness of the night.

Fear gripped her like a thief in the dark. Exposed and vulnerable, she held her breath as the wind blew sand over her bare skin. Morbid scenarios sabotaged her thoughts, playing out like some creepy horror flick. Shivering uncontrollably, she stood and screamed into the night, "You're just gonna leave me here, you jerk?!"

"Ce-cil-ia?"

"Who's there?"

The clouds had rolled in with the impending storm and snuffed out the starlights, leaving the night pitch-black and daunting. Unable to see anyone, she scrambled to get her clothes on. "Don't ya know I'm scared of the dark?" she cried.

"Ce-cil-ia?"

"This isn't funny! Who's there?" *Maybe it's nothing. The wind's howling, and the waves are loud crashing against the shore,* she thought as she bolted down the beach. The tailwind seemed to push her along. Every time she inhaled the salty air, her lungs felt like they would collapse.

Up ahead, a glimmer of light pierced the fog-laden night. Cecilia ran towards it, hoping it came from the beach parking lot where she had left her car.

She groped near the shoreline until she stood before the shadow of the stairs. A man's hand reached for her. Falling forward with the next step, she grabbed hold as he led her up the stairway to the parking lot.

"You shouldn't be all alone on the beach after dark," he said as he released her hand and started to walk away.

"Hey, what's your name?"

The stranger didn't answer.

Cecilia fumbled to pull her keys from her pocket. When she looked up, the man had vanished.

"Oh, my god!" She hurried to the car, jammed her key into the ignition switch, and pulled out of the parking lot in a frenzy. *"Who was he? Where'd he come from?"* She glanced into the rearview mirror and confirmed that no shadowy figures had moved. Cecilia's pulse accelerated in tandem with the speed of her car as she headed home.

3

WITH HER MIND still haunted by the relentless replay of the night's events, Cecilia managed to slip into the house unnoticed. Tiptoeing, she peered into the den and found Mama wrapped in her bathrobe and curled up on the couch, engrossed in her favorite TV show, *Jeopardy*. Daddy was asleep in his recliner, with an occasional head bob whenever he snored.

Great! she thought, hoping to make it to the bathroom without any confrontations from the two of them.

She froze when the bathroom door squeaked.

"Is that you, Cecilia?" Mama yelled out.

"Yes, ma'am. I'm gonna get a shower and go to bed," she called back as she closed the bathroom door and turned on the water, hoping her answer would satisfy Mama.

She undressed, letting her clothes fall to the floor. Sean's scent lingered on her skin. Waves breaking and lapping the shoreline played in her head as the warm shower water splashed on her trembling body.

*Why did I do that? Was I that desperate? For what? He got what he wanted, but did I? What **did** I expect to get from someone I barely knew?* Cecilia covered her mouth with the palm of her hand to barricade the groans she felt trying to erupt. *And who was that man? Why did he help me?* Feeling dizzy, she grabbed hold of the shower bar to keep from falling and lowered herself into the tub.

"I'm so stupid!" she sobbed.

Daddy banged on the bathroom door. "Hurry up in there! Stop running so much water! Do you wanna pay the water bill this month?"

"No, Daddy," she whispered, turning off the water. She got up, grabbed a towel, and began drying herself. The shame of the night washed over her as she stood before the mirror naked. Repulsed and consumed with fatigue from the emotional roller coaster, she managed to slip on her nightgown and crawl into bed.

Tossing and turning like a sailboat ravaged by the storm, she ached for someone to rescue her. But there was no one. The boat had capsized, leaving her to drown in an ocean of fear.

*H*E NEVER TRIED *to find me.*
Waiting…
Days turned into weeks— No period.

"Mama, I don't feel well."

"Any fever?" Mama asked while putting clothes in the washer.

"Don't think so," she said, holding her hand to her forehead.

Mama turned and stared at her.

"Have you started your period?"

"No, Mama." Cecilia looked down, averting her eyes.

What if she tells Daddy?

"How long?!"

Cecilia barely got the words out, "Seven weeks, maybe. Mama, I–"

"Shhh! Call Josh and stay with him for a while. Do you understand me?"

"Mama—"

"Shhh! Go ahead and call him! Call him now!" Mama exited the room, slamming the door behind her.

Cecilia flinched and hurried to her bedroom. Her brother, Josh, had joined the army after high school and would come home for visits with a present in hand. She felt safe and protected when he was around, but he wasn't around *enough*.

How can I do this? What do I say to him? What will he think about me?

Scared and alone, she made the call. Josh's wife, Ana, answered.

"Hi, Ana. Is Josh around?"

"Hey Cece, just a moment."

She could hear her brother in the background asking Ana who it was before taking the phone. "Cece, what's up?"

"Josh." Cecilia's voice cracked.

"What's going on? Are you okay?"

"I'm 99% positive I'm pregnant," she said, choking on the words.

Silence.

"Have ya told anyone?"

"Mama knows, but she doesn't wanna talk about it. She told me I needed to stay with you for a while. I'm scared. If Daddy finds out, he'll kill me! You know he will."

Daddy was a hardworking man. And a hard-drinking man. He always had a pint of vodka in hand's reach in his truck and at home. While other daddies tucked their daughters in at night, Cecilia hoped her daddy would stay away.

"Was this your first time?"

"Yes," she lied, not wanting to tell the truth. Her shame was already hitting a toxic level.

"Are you sure no one knows?"

Is he judging me now? Would he think I'm a better person if I'd only had sex with one person? Was he more concerned about my reputation than with Daddy's rage?

"No one knows."

"Well, don't tell anyone, and I'll get back to you after I talk to Ana."

"Okay but please call back soon. I'm scared, Josh."

Hanging up, Cecilia buried her face in her pillow and sobbed until she couldn't breathe. Echoes of "shhh" resounded as she came up for air. After gaining her composure she found the Pregnancy Testing Center's number on her phone and called them.

Don't tell anyone. Are you sure no one knows? Josh's voice reverberated louder and louder in her mind. She quickly hung up *before* anyone could answer.

I NEED AIR. *I'VE gotta get out of this house before I suffocate. Daddy'll be home soon, and I can't deal with him right now.*

"Mama, I'm gonna go to Julie's house for a while," she lied.

"Okay, but be back before dark."

Cecilia grabbed her keys and left. The distance between her house and *his* was only a few miles, yet their paths had never crossed before *that* night. He was nineteen and had just graduated from high school, while she was sixteen.

With thoughts running rampent, she drove toward his house where they had first met.

His girlfriend's probably there. Who am I kidding? Besides that, he left me in the dark to fend for myself.

She continued to hear Josh's voice in her head.

***Don't** tell anyone!*

She pulled onto the shoulder of the road and sat while the traffic zoomed by. Cecilia rested her head on the steering wheel as tears flooded her cheeks.

"Pregnant? Really?" she screamed, pounding the dashboard with her fist.

Once the traffic cleared, she spun the car around and went home, trying to see through the tears streaming down her face.

A glimpse of the sun setting warmed her soul. The gentle wind blew in the open car window as she noted the sea oats dancing in the wind. Peace embraced her like a loving hug until reality shook her soul like a tornado, demolishing everything in its path. The sobs became louder as the chaos in her mind grew fierce. *What **am** I gonna do? Somebody help me!*

The inconsolable cries left her breathless as she turned into the gas station near her house.

"Okay, just breathe, just breathe," she repeated. "Get it together now! You can't go in like this."

Pulling into the driveway, her muscles twitched, and her chest tightened as she stepped out of the car and walked into the house. She could hear Daddy shouting cuss words at Mama through the closed utility room door. Frozen with fear and dread of what the night might bring, she took a deep breath and exhaled. The scars on her hand from the last time she tried to intervene warned her not to get too close.

"Oh god," she cried while propping herself up against the wall. She began to rock back and forth until Mama's hysterical screams forced her to move.

As she opened the door into the hallway, she found Mama on the floor shielding her face with her arms as Daddy stood over her, ready to strike.

"Stop! Stop it!" Cecilia yelled as a surge of adrenaline flowed through her veins.

Daddy turned and lunged at her. "What did you say?" He managed a tight smile that didn't reach his eyes and drew back to slap her.

Mama screamed again.

He cracked his neck from side to side, muttered more cuss words, turned, and walked toward the den.

"I'm okay, Cecilia. Go to your room now," Mama pleaded.

The walls reverberated with the booming television volume, making it difficult to hear anything she said.

"Let me help you up." Taking her hand, Cecilia managed to get her to the bathroom. She took a wet washcloth and patted the blood oozing from Mama's forehead.

"What happened?" she asked while applying pressure to the cut to stop the bleeding.

"He shoved me, and I hit the corner of the door. That's all. It's nothing. It's already stopped bleeding now," Mama explained as she took the washcloth from Cecilia.

"Well, at least let me put some antibiotic ointment and a band-aid on it."

"I'm okay. He'll be asleep in a minute. You go on to bed now. I'm alright."

With a painful lump in her throat, Cecilia shook her head. She went down the hall and saw Daddy asleep in his chair with drool running down the corner of his mouth.

Once in her bedroom, she secured a chair against the door and crawled into bed with her clothes on, just in case she had to run out during the night. Living there taught her one thing: always plan a way to escape.

"Why Mama? Why do you stay with him?" Cecilia cried. "You have to know what he's done to me. I *heard* you talking one night. I heard you tell him to leave me alone. I was so young, Mama. Why didn't you help me?" Afraid of waking Daddy, she buried her face in the pillow until her well of tears had run dry.

Mama married him when she was eighteen. Daddy was twenty-five and still in the Army. Josh was born five years later. Seven years after that, Mama ended up pregnant with *her*.

"Did you even *want* me, Mama? Did *you want* to have an abortion? Is that why you want me to have one?" Cecilia teared up again, thinking of the seed growing inside her.

6

HEARING HER NAME again, she woke to see Nurse Lucy peering down at her.

"Cecilia, this is Dr. Horton."

A tall, slender man with pepper gray hair and a receding hairline stared over the glasses that slid down his nose.

"Looks like you were working a little too hard in the heat yesterday. You were dehydrated when you got here and barely conscious. We gave you IV fluids, checked your vital signs, and did some blood work. We also did a pregnancy test, which was positive. Were you aware that you're pregnant?" he asked.

"Yes." Her suspicion was now confirmed.

"Your blood work returned normal, and I'm going to send you home today. You need to start taking better care of yourself. I suggest you not garden in the heat of the day and make sure you drink enough water." After scribbling on a pad, he tore a piece loose and handed her a prescription for prenatal vitamins. "Get this filled at the drugstore and make an appointment with your doctor as soon as possible." Closing the chart with a snap, he turned and made his exit.

She crumpled the prescription in her hands without Lucy seeing. *Sure, if I get this filled within twenty miles of my house, the whole town will know.*

"I'll get your discharge papers together while you're getting dressed. Your brother called and said he's on his way. By the way," Lucy continued, "your guardian went to the business office and took care of the bill. They said it was paid in full—cash! He asked them to let you know because he didn't want you to worry about *anything*, especially the cost of your hospital stay. That sure was nice of him."

"Oh, and don't forget your beautiful plant with that gorgeous bloom. He said it was for your garden. I'll be right back," Lucy said as she left the room.

Paid my bill? Who is he, and what does he know about me? A plant for my garden? What does he want from me? Cecilia recalled the night at the beach when the man pulled her up the steps. *Could it be him? What's going on?*

She moved toward the window and stared at the crimson blooms. Tears trickled down her face.

"Garden? I don't have a garden."

THESE CLOTHES ARE so dirty. I'll never be able to get these grass stains out! Why did he help me? I wish he had just left me there!

Cecilia heard a soft knock on the door before she saw Mama enter the hospital room.

"I thought you could use some fresh clothes," she said while handing her a small tote bag. "Joshua called yesterday and told me you were here and a friend was staying with you. Your dad thinks you were at Julie's studying for a test. I would've come last night but didn't know what to tell your him. When I got home yesterday, I saw the holes you dug in the backyard for the garden, and I tried to cover them up before he got home. You know how angry he would've been if the yard was left like that."

"I don't care about the yard or what Daddy thinks about it. I *needed* you here, Mama!"

"Well, I *have* to care about what he thinks! I'm the one–"

"Mama," Cecilia interrupted, "I'm pregnant."

Mama's face hardened. The bulging veins in her temples looked as if they would explode any moment. "Are you sure?"

"Yes, they did a blood test."

"Who is it? Who did this to you? Was it the friend that stayed with you last night?" Her voice escalated with every question. "You need to stay with Joshua and get *it* taken care of! Do you hear me? Your daddy will *kill* that boy!"

Lucy came in before Mama could say anything more.

"Hello. Mrs. Evans, I presume?"

"Yes," Mama said, rather coldly.

"The doctor has discharged Cecilia, and I'm about to review the discharge instructions with her. I'm glad you're here to listen. We tried to call you earlier. Will you be taking her home now? Her brother called and said *he* was on the way."

"No, he'll be picking her up."

Are you too embarrassed to be seen with me, Mama? Do you even care how I'm doing or how I got to the hospital?

Lucy went over the discharge instructions with them. Mama signed and promptly left after whispering in Cecilia's ear to go by the house and get some more clothes for her stay at Josh's.

Mama didn't seem worried about anything but me taking care of it.

"Do you have any questions?" Lucy asked.

"No, ma'am." Her phone buzzed with a text from Ana saying they would pick her up in the circle by the main entrance in ten minutes.

Cecilia quickly texted back: I'LL BE READY!

"My brother just texted and said he'll be in the circle in a few minutes."

"Collect your things then, and I'll go get a wheelchair."

Cecilia went to the window and scooped up the plant. She wanted to know more about this *guardian* but kept quiet, afraid of raising a red flag if she asked questions.

Lucy insisted Cecilia ride to the front door in the wheelchair. She gladly sat down while Lucy wheeled her out, still babbling about hospital policy.

Once outside, she sat on the bench as a mother and her newborn baby were being picked up. A blue SUV pulled up, and a young man quickly jumped out to open the door for them. He proudly started taking pictures. Lucy offered to take a picture of the three of them.

Cecilia sat staring as she imagined how difficult it would be to carry her baby home. As her left hand glided over her abdomen, she shook it as though to release whatever she was holding on to.

"God, please don't let anyone see me. Please, God," she pleaded under her breath. Cecilia only called on Him when she needed something. She had a love-hate relationship with God ever since the neighbor had dragged her to a Sunday school class. She wanted to know the good Father they talked about but doubted she could ever trust someone called *Father*.

Her thoughts were disrupted by the sound of Josh's red Chevy backfiring. Ana opened the door, and Cecilia crawled into the back seat.

"Take care of yourself," Lucy said while turning the wheelchair back toward the hospital door.

"Yes, ma'am," Cecilia said, wanting to escape quickly.

"Hey, you alright?" Josh asked.

"That's a loaded question! I guess so. They're not keeping me."

"Last night, a man from the hospital called and told us you passed out in the heat. He assured us you were okay but said they were going to keep you overnight and release you today. He wanted me to let Mama know. I called and told her what he said and that we'd pick you up and run by the house to get your clothes so you could stay with us for a while since school's out."

"I bet she was happy with that news!" Cecilia said, rolling her eyes.

"Yeah, I guess so. Did she go to the hospital last night?"

"No. Mama's too ashamed of me." Cecilia's lip began to quiver.

"This is too much drama!"

"Well, I'm sorry about that, Josh! It is what it is! I guess you think I'm a *slut* too!

"I never said that!"

"You didn't have to!"

"Just talk to me and tell me what's going on!" Josh's voice grew louder with every word. Ana poked him in the side and motioned for him to calm down..

Cecilia exploded. "I was digging holes in the backyard trying to plant a stupid garden and passed out! Mama was at the store! I don't remember anything after that, or maybe I don't wanna remember. I'm pregnant, and I don't know what to do!" she yelled. "I'm tired of everyone telling me to be quiet because they don't want to hear about it like that's gonna make *it* go away! Shhh! Shhh, is all I hear!"

Shocked by the sudden outburst, Josh and Ana got quiet.

Cecilia's stomach growled so loudly it broke the mounting tension.

"**And** I'm starving!" she yelled.

"Heads up," he said, throwing a Ray's burger bag across the seat to her.

Cecilia opened the bag and quickly closed it after the smell of greasy food wafted up her nostrils. "Thanks, but no thanks," she said, tossing it back to the front seat. "I'd rather be hungry than puking."

Josh and Ana remained quiet. It wasn't long before he pulled into her driveway so she could get her clothes.

"I'll be quick since he's not home yet. Maybe we'll miss him," she said, crawling out of the backseat.

"Do you want me to go in with you?"

Cecilia looked at him and shook her head no, not wanting to risk the chance of Daddy coming home and them getting into an altercation. It didn't take much for Josh to tick him off, especially if Daddy had been drinking, which he usually did on the way home from work. She thought about the night he hit Josh in the head with a board when he tried sneaking back in the window after a ballgame. He wouldn't stop. He just kept beating him. Her insides began to quiver. *Why did he hurt him like that?* Cecilia began to tremble. *Why never seemed relevant.*

"No, I'll be back in a minute." She ran up the steps and entered through the back door, hoping to get in and out as quickly as possible. She sat her new plant on the dresser and paused. "My mysterious angel plant. You need a name," she said, examining the velvety leaves again. "Sophia means wisdom, and I sure could use some right now! That's it, from now on you will be *Sophia.*" In an effort to escape Mama's interrogation, she quickly gathered some clothes, and her newfound friend and hurried out of the room only to find Mama lurking on the other side of the door.

"I thought I heard someone. You seem to be in a hurry."

"Josh and Ana are waiting for me in the car. I just came to get my clothes. I was hoping to leave before Daddy got home."

"I guess you were."

Cecilia stared at her. "Isn't this what you wanted?'

"Yes," she said without blinking.

"I guess they'll bring me home when it's all over with."

Mama noticed the plant tucked under Cecilia's arm.

"Where'd that plant come from?" she asked.

"Someone at the hospital gave it to me."

"I've never seen one like that." Mama loved plants and working in her flower garden.

Cecilia stood still and quiet.

"Alright then. You go on now and give my love to Joshua."

Really? He could do no wrong in her eyes, or maybe she felt guilty for how Daddy treated him. "Sure Mama, I'll do that!"

"Mama loves you, Josh," Cecilia said as she threw her bag in the back seat and got in.

As they left the driveway on their way to Josh and Ana's tiny apartment in Virginia, rain began to fall. Before they rounded the first curve, Ana announced they had scheduled Cecilia an appointment with the Women's Alternative Care Clinic at nine in the morning to discuss her options. The awkward silence that followed was only interrupted by the windshield wipers rubbing against the glass when the rain slowed. Cecilia held her stomach every time the truck tires hit a bump in the road. When they got to Josh and Ana's one-bedroom apartment, she washed her face and slid under the blanket on the couch in the living room. Pulling the covers over her head, she whispered into the darkness, "Sophia, tell me this is a dream, and I'm gonna wake up in the morning and *it* will all be over with."

7

Cecilia woke early the following morning to the sound of Ana shutting the door on her way to work. Rolling onto her back, she muttered, "Guess it's no dream." A groan escaped her lips as a wave of nausea swept over her. *I can't do this. Maybe if I stay still, it'll pass.*

The next thing she knew, the sun was streaming through the blinds lighting up the room. Cecilia reluctantly dragged herself out of bed, wrapping a blanket around her shoulders as she shuffled toward the kitchen to find Josh bustling about.

"Morning, Josh."

"Morning, Cece."

"We have that appointment today to see if we can get some help," Josh said as he brewed the coffee.

Help? I know what kind of help, she thought as she ran to the bathroom and held her head over the toilet.

Josh was quickly behind her. "What can I do? Do you need anything?"

"No, just give me a minute."

She rinsed her mouth at the sink, combed her hair, and splashed her face with cold water. She had slept in her jogging pants and shirt the night before. Grabbing her sweatshirt from the hanger on the back of the bathroom door, she pulled it over her head, leaving the hood up. Her swollen and bloodshot eyes glared back as she peered into the mirror.

Everything's moving too fast. I feel so rushed. Now, you say someone's gonna help me. Tell me options. Right, like I have options?

Cecilia knew the Alternative Care Clinic was an abortion clinic. That's precisely what Mama wanted; *just take care of it!*

She thought back to her hospital stay. It was all a blur.

Cecilia went back to the kitchen table where Josh was drinking his coffee.

"Hey, *who* called you from the hospital?" she asked.

"I don't recall him giving his name. He said to let Mama know you were there. I figured you had given the hospital my number because you didn't want them to call your house in case Dad answered the phone."

"I didn't give *anyone* your name or number," she said sternly.

"Then *who* called me?"

"Good question."

NINE O'CLOCK. THE time was drawing near.

Josh and Cecilia didn't speak as he drove to the middle of town. "This is it. I'll let you out and go park the car."

Cecilia hesitated before opening the truck door and glancing back at Josh. Her stomach churned as she stepped onto the curb. She walked up to the white brick building and stood before the large revolving door leading into the clinic. Over the door read **Women's Alternative Care** in big, bold black letters. She noticed the large clay flower pot beside the door had turned over, spilling out dirt and red geraniums. The pot was cracked, and several broken pieces were mixed with the dirt. She stooped down, stuck the roots of the flowers back into the soil, and brushed the dirt from her hands. Her throat tightened. *I want to run away from here, but where and to whom do I run?*

Josh emerged from the parking lot, took hold of her hand, and led the way into the abortion clinic.

Cecilia signed in at the front desk. She was promptly called back by a young woman dressed in lime-colored scrubs whose hair was pulled up into a ponytail, showcasing multiple earrings that lined the rim of her ears.

"Hello, my name's Lindsey. Have a seat. What's your first and last name, please?"

"Cecilia Evans."

"When was the first day of your last period?"

"April 15th."

"Okay. I'll need a urine sample so we can do a pregnancy test," she said, handing her a cup with her name on it and pointing to the restroom. "Put it on the counter when you've finished and then sit out front. We'll call you back shortly."

The whole process seemed surreal. *Is this happening to me?* Cecilia thought while doing what Lindsey instructed.

It wasn't long before someone else came to the door and called her name. "Cecilia, I'm Mrs. Parks. Come into my office and have a seat, please. The pregnancy test was positive, and according to your last menstrual period date, you're about nine weeks pregnant." The counselor talked fast. "Do you plan on continuing with your pregnancy?"

"I'd like to know my options," she said, remembering Ana and Josh discussing *options*.

"We can talk about that. You do have some options."

I don't think I'm going to like any of them!

"Number one, you can give birth and become a parent. Is the father involved?"

"No, ma'am." *The father? You mean the asshole. What a joke! I let him use me. Oh wait, I'm the absolute joke. It was my fault. I won't make that mistake again! He left me there all alone in the dark. He didn't even have the decency to help me get back to my car.*

"Cecilia, did you hear me?"

"I'm sorry, what did you say?"

"Do you have someone to support you and a baby financially, or can you do so on your own?"

"No," Cecilia said, wringing her hands.

"Another option is an abortion. The doctor uses some medical instruments and, with a mild suction, removes the pregnancy tissue."

Pregnancy tissue? That's right. It's not a baby.

"Adoption is also an option," the counselor continued. "The child will be permanently placed with another family or individual after birth. Do you have any questions?"

"No questions," Cecilia said without blinking. "I wanna have an abortion."

"Alright then, I'll need you to look over these papers and sign on the yellow highlighted lines."

Cecilia looked over the possible risks during the procedure and took a deep breath.

The counselor caught a glimpse of Cecilia's furrowed brow and responded immediately. "Any possible complications are rare."

Cecilia shook her head as if to understand, yet all the words were blurry as tears skimmed her eyes. She quickly signed the rest of the papers without reading them and returned them to the counselor, wondering how many girls would sign on the yellow line today.

"Your sister-in-law took care of getting your mother's signature just in case you made this decision."

Cecilia's eyes widened. "Really?"

"Yes, it's all been taken care of. It's nine o' clock now. We have a cancellation for three o'clock this afternoon if you'd like to return then."

Too numb to answer, she nodded.

Can't you do it now? I don't wanna wait. I don't wanna think about this anymore. What if I can't do this? Somebody, tell me not to. Somebody, help me. Please, somebody.

She remained quiet, choking back the words her mind dictated, but her heart screamed.

"Have you eaten anything today?" the counselor asked.

"No," Cecilia nervously blurted out. "I haven't eaten anything today."

"Well, don't eat anything until after the procedure. You'll be here a couple of hours afterward. The procedure itself only takes about five to ten minutes. You should be ready to go around five-ish. When you return, we'll give you a mild sedative to help you be more comfortable. Are you allergic to anything?"

"No."

"And Cecilia? This *is* what **you** want?" the counselor asked, never looking up from her paperwork.

"Yes."

"Okay then," she said, getting up from her desk. "I'll take you to the ultrasound technician. She will scan your abdomen and pelvis area with some gel and a probe. We need to make sure your dates are correct and everything looks good before performing the procedure. The gel is a little cold, but it doesn't hurt."

Well, Mama, you won't have to worry about Daddy now or be embarrassed because nobody will know. It'll be our secret. And Daddy, you won't have another child around the house to hurt. After today, it'll all be over with. I'll have the summer off and can finish school. Life will go on as usual... Or will it?

"We'll see you at three o'clock this afternoon. You may pay on your way out with a money order or a major credit card," she said, parting her lips with a brief smile as she closed the door to the ultrasound room and left.

*Wow. That wasn't what I was expecting. What **did** I expect? Someone to be warm and fuzzy? Someone to talk me out of having an abortion? One thing is for sure: She let me know I'd be paying upfront! There will be no billing later for this procedure.*

A knock on the door came before a young woman in scrubs entered the room.

"Hi, I'm Lisa, and I'm gonna do your ultrasound now."

Cecilia watched as the woman rolled the machine closer to the table, instructing her to lie down, lift her shirt, and lower her jogging pants. The tech had the screen facing away from her so Cecilia couldn't see anything as she continued to rub the probe over her abdomen.

"Mrs. Parks was right; that is some cold gel," Cecilia interjected, trying to break the silence.

"It sure is."

The tech never asked if she wanted to see the screen, and Cecilia didn't dare ask.

I guess it's better if I don't see.

"All done now," the tech said as she wiped the gel off Cecilia's stomach. "You may leave."

She quickly tidied herself up, left the room, and found Josh sitting in the lobby.

"We have to be back at three today. I need to pay now," Cecilia said.

Josh went to the desk, took out his credit card, and returned with a receipt.

"You look pale. Do you need some water or to sit down for a minute?" he asked.

"I'm fine. Let's leave. It smells musty in here, and I don't wanna throw up."

"How bout we go to the park around the corner and hang out?"

Cecilia nodded her head yes, wanting fresh air. "I'll pay you back."

"No worries."

A barrage of thoughts prevailed like a massive tidal wave chasing her down as she tried to justify her decision. *This isn't a baby. They said* **the** *pregnancy tissue. It has to be okay. It's legal now. I'm not going down some dark alley. This isn't a crime. Mama won't be happy unless I do this. Nobody will have to know. They'd all want to know who the father was. They said mild suction. Is that gonna hurt? I'm scared! I feel nauseous. I won't feel nauseous anymore. Why do I want to cry? I feel like I'm gonna fall apart. I don't wanna fall apart! STOP IT! I have to do this.*

Walking through the revolving door, knowing she would be back, the war continued between her head and her heart. More concerned she would be found out, her head was winning the fight.

Josh and Cecilia didn't speak as he drove to the park. Once they arrived, he lay on the park bench, and she sat on the hill watching baby ducks paddle behind their mother. Lying back, she lost herself in the pure, white, fluffy clouds above as she began creating animal objects like she did as a young child. A massive fish and a dog were painted across the sky until the clouds moved, changing her picture. Time stood still. It felt like three o'clock would never come. Attempting to escape, she closed her eyes, and took a deep breath.

What do you want, Cecilia? What do **you** *want? Cecilia, what do you* **want?** The tidal wave carried her away into a deep sleep as she surrendered to its assault.

Abruptly, she woke to hear Josh calling her. Walking to the car, she heard an ice cream truck's bell ringing nearby and saw small children gathering for a treat. Their laughter faded as she shut the car door.

Would she ever laugh again? *Oh Mama, where are you? Hold me, Mama, and make everything okay.*

"Cecilia?"

Taking a moment to get her bearings, she replied, "Yes?"

"Are you okay with this?"

"I guess. It's the best choice," she said tearfully, feeling like it was the *only* choice.

"Ana's meeting us at the clinic, and we'll go out to eat when *this* is all over."

"Fine," she said. Something felt wrong as she thought about going to eat as a celebration of no longer being pregnant.

Within a few minutes, they were back at the clinic. Cecilia stood staring at the revolving doors. Heart pounding, she pushed open the door into the facility and stepped through, knowing she would exit the revolving door void of...*it.*

After checking in, they took her to a room where she was asked again. "Cecilia, do you have any questions?"

"No."

"I need to get your blood pressure and take your temperature," the nurse said while wrapping a cuff around her arm. "Are you allergic to any medications?"

"No."

The nurse proceeded to hand her a small cup with several pills and another filled with water.

"Well, I'm not allergic to anything that I know of," she said, downing the pills with one gulp.

"Okay, follow me, and I'll take you to the next waiting room."

Cecilia found a chair in the corner and sat down. She counted fifteen others waiting. Some were chatting, and others were looking down or out the window. In the far corner was a lady and a man, appearing to be in their late thirties. She found herself scrutinizing them. *Why would they do this? They have each other.* Faint from not eating and nauseous from taking the pills on an empty stomach, she laid her head on her arm as it cradled the back of the chair.

Maybe, this is wrong...

9

THE CLOCK ON the wall ticked away like a bomb, ready to explode any minute. She wanted to run again but made no effort. Instead she sat. And sat. More time passed.

The door opened.

"Cecilia?" a nurse called.

She stood and followed, allowing time to carry her into the procedure room.

The sterile-looking room felt dirty. Cecilia's eyes were fixed on the foot stirrups of the table.

"I'm cold," she said, never breaking her gaze.

"I'll bring you a blanket, but first, put this gown on and tie it in the back. Here are some socks for you, too. I'll be right back."

Cecilia went to the sink and washed her hands, scrubbing them with hot water and soap until they were red and stung. *It doesn't matter how hard I scrub. This kind of dirt never comes off.* "I'm sorry baby, tissue, whatever you are," she said, cupping her hands over her stomach.

Dropping her clothes on the floor, she stepped into an oversized gown and walked toward the bed, going through the motions while others directed the scene.

"Death. A heartbeat stops. Not mine, but that of the pregnancy tissue," she whispered. "Mama, I wish *you* had *aborted me.*"

CECILIA HEARD A knock on the door. It opened.

The nurse came in, followed by a man in scrubs.

"Hello, young lady. I'm Dr. Bradshaw, and I'll be doing your procedure today."

Black, framed glasses and a scrub hat covering his hair with a mask hiding his face made it difficult for Cecilia to tell what he looked like.

Things began to move fast again, too fast.

"Let me help get your feet up in the stirrups now," the nurse said, bringing her body closer to the end of the exam table while the doctor perched himself on a stool between her legs. He mumbled something to the nurse, and Cecilia watched her turn the suction machine on.

Cognizant of everything going on but feeling sleepy from the pain medicine, she softly asked, "Is this gonna hurt?"

"You should be fine," he said. "I'm going to apply some numbing medication to your cervix."

Her eyes were drawn to him talking to the nurse, but she couldn't make out what they were saying.

"We're going to get started now," he said in a louder voice.

She took another deep breath when she saw him reach for a silver instrument.

"This is going to be a little cold."

Wincing, she felt the cold metal instrument entering her vagina before she had time to say, "Wait." She felt like a lone child on a never-ending merry-go-round, going round and round. She gazed at the suction canister as blood entered the tube. Not wanting to see the *tissue*, she squeezed her eyes shut.

"I'm going to puke. I need to sit up," she cried after several minutes of intense cramping. "I can't stop shaking. It hurts!"

"Hold her legs still!" the doctor shouted.

"Listen to me now," the nurse said in an even, steady voice while staring Cecilia straight in the face. "You have to be still. This'll be over in a few minutes. I need you to take some slow, deep breaths through your nose and blow them out through your mouth."

Cecilia closed her eyes and felt her legs spread wider. Her head swirling, she wanted off this merry-go-round, yet she dared not move. All she could hear now was the sound of suction mimicking the undertow of the waves, pulling the life inside of her out. And then, the noise stopped.

"Okay now, all done," Dr. Bradshaw said as he peeled his gloves off, dropped them in the trash can, and left the room without saying anything more.

And just like that, it's over. She lay staring at the ceiling tiles as the nurse fussed with the suction canister, muttering something under her breath.

What is she saying? I hope she's not talking to me. I have nothing to say, she thought while constantly twirling her hair.

"Cecilia? Can you hear me? I want you to sit up on the side of the bed, and I'll help you with your panties and a pad. You may experience some more cramping. There's a room at the end of the hall on the right with cots where you can lie down until your bleeding has slowed up and you're…"

"I need to go. I need to go to the bathroom." Stepping into the panty and pad get-up, she allowed the nurse to steady her as she walked to the bathroom a few feet away. She kept her eyes fixed on the bathroom door trying to escape the canister filled with blood and tissue.

"I'm cold."

"I'll help you get your clothes on after you use the bathroom." The nurse proceeded to talk as Cecilia lowered herself onto the toilet seat. "You may have some bleeding for the next ten days to two weeks. Call us back if the bleeding becomes heavier or longer than three weeks. You may also experience some cramping, like a period. They'll go over some more things before you leave."

The more she talked, the more withdrawn Cecilia became.

"Let me help you back to the table now," the nurse said after giving her a new pad. She retrieved Cecilia's jogging pants and sweatshirt from the chair and held onto her as she stepped in. "I'll be back to walk you to the recovery area in a minute. After recovery, your ride will be able to take you home. Just take it easy the next few days. Cecilia, you were a brave girl," the nurse said as she opened the door to leave.

Cecilia heard what sounded like a stampede of horses galloping down the hall before everything became as quiet as a midnight graveyard. Too quiet.

"I've gotta get outta here," she said while calling Josh from her cell phone to pick her up at the front door.

Faint and weak, she managed to stand up. "I better not pass out. I'm getting out of this place now!" She grabbed the bag they had given her to put her clothes in and threw the pads in before she opened the door. Everyone must have been busy silencing the screams because the halls were empty. No need to pay. They ensured the fee was paid and the paperwork was completed *before* the procedure. Cecilia gripped her stomach, hoping to ease the pain. With her throat closing, she yearned for a breath of fresh air.

Making her way through the revolving door, her hand touched *another woman's* hand through the glass, and their eyes exchanged a brief knowing. One stepped out, and the other stepped in. A great wave of sorrow for the other woman swept over Cecilia as she anticipated her having the *same* ride on the *same* merry-go-round.

"Hey, we would've come in for you," Josh said as he got out of the car to help her into the back seat.

She looked at him with tear-filled eyes.

"It's gonna be alright," Josh said.

Wiping her eyes, she nodded.

Josh closed her door and jumped back in the driver's seat. He and Ana glanced at one another with quizzical eyes.

"Hey, Cecilia," Josh said.

"Yeah."

"Knock knock."

"Are you kidding me, Josh?"

"No! Knock knock!" he repeated.

"Who's there?"

"Lettuce!"

"Lettuce who?"

"Lettuce get outta here!"

Cecilia saw him peering at her in the driver's mirror and managed half a smile. "Yeah, lettuce, get outta here!"

He had always been a master at knock-knock jokes whenever he came home from the Army and found her in tears.

Josh winked at her and sped away like he was in the Indy 500 and had just been given the green light. After seeing Ana cringe and grab the door handle, he tapped the brakes to slow things down.

Cecilia closed her eyes during the ride to the restaurant and tried to escape the nightmare that had been playing out since that night on the beach.

A T THE RESTAURANT, Cecilia sat at the table with the red checkered tablecloth and twirled her spaghetti around the fork while the strong smell of garlic and basil turned her stomach. The red marinara sauce triggered thoughts of the suction canister filling with blood. With sweat beading up on her forehead, she laid her fork down on the table and looked at Ana with pleading eyes.

"Do you want some help to the bathroom?" Ana asked while wiping the sweat from Cecilia's face and neck with her white napkin.

"Yes, please." Cecilia made her way into the bathroom stall and locked the door. Sitting on the toilet, she wept while blood mingled with urine flowed into the bowl. *What had the nurse done with the canister of blood and pregnancy tissue? Was it flushed down the toilet?*

"Cecilia, I'm here," Ana whispered through the door.

"I wanna go home," she cried, coming out of the bathroom stall.

Ana held her in her arms until she felt her start to pull away.

"Are you able to walk to the car?"

"Yes."

It was a sunny day. Cecilia noticed children playing on the merry-go-round as they passed the elementary school. She looked away and closed her eyes. The warm sunshine radiated through the window while the pain medicine she had been given at the clinic helped her doze off for the ride to Josh and Ana's.

Back at the apartment, Josh and Ana went about their everyday lives: work, friends, activities. The week was ending, and she knew it was time to go home and face Mama.

Oh, Mama! You could have called. I guess I should have died too, Mama. Maybe that's what you wanted. Or maybe, just maybe, you wanted me to suffer enough so this would never happen again. Well, you don't have to worry about that anymore, Mama. I won't ever forget this.

Wednesday came. Mama met them at the back door. "Thanks, Joshua, for bringing Cecilia home. I hope she wasn't too much trouble."

Aren't you going to ask me about my time at Josh's? I suppose you don't want to know, do you, Mama?

Josh kissed Mama and Cecilia on the forehead. "Cecilia can come back anytime she wants to!" he said, waving goodbye.

"I'm glad you're back. Get your dirty clothes together and put them in the wash."

"Sure."

Closing her bedroom door, Cecilia threw her bag on the floor and put Sophia on the desk by the window. "You're my angel plant and my best friend. At least I know *you'll* listen to me! And God, if perhaps you're listening from somewhere up there, I want you to know something. I promise this won't ever happen again." *As if bargaining with Him would make everything all right.* Deep down inside, she wasn't sure this *could* be made right.

How can I ever forgive myself for what I've done? Yes, it's over... No baby to show or get in anyone's way. So, why does my heart feel like it's bleeding?

To AVOID ALL unnecessary contact with Mama, Cecilia kept her phone close and waited for someone to call and take her away. Today was her lucky day.

"Hey Chris, yeah, the river sounds great. Can you pick me up? Ten? Sure, I'll be ready."

It should be safe to swim now. It's been six weeks since that day, and the spotting has stopped.

In the middle of the week, Chris's parents were at work and wouldn't be home or at the river. Word must have gotten out because the dirt road to the cottage was lined with cars.

"How many people did you invite over?" asked Cecilia.

"You know how it is. I told a few people, and they told a few more, and here we are." Chris had asked her out a few times before school ended, and by the way he looked at her, she could tell he wanted to be more than just friends.

"Well, sure looks like a lot of beer drinking and partying going on here!" she laughed.

"Yeah, and the boat is ready to go! Grab your towel, and let's jump on before they take off again! There's Jake. He sees us. Oh yeah, he's waving a bottle of tequila!"

Jake handed her a shot glass before she got on the boat. "Glad to see ya, Cece!"

"Okay, let the fun begin," she said while downing the tequila and climbing onto the boat. She barely sat down before he handed her another one.

"Chase it with this," Chris said, handing her a joint.

It didn't take long for the tequila to kick in. Smiling, she reached up to kiss him. "You're so nice to me."

"I love you, Cece."

"I only let my close friends call me Cece." He pulled her close and wrapped the beach towel around both of them.

She laid her head on his chest and could feel his heart beating. His skin was warm and tanned.

I wish I could love you, Chris, but I'm not sure I can ever really love anyone.

Lifting her chin, he lowered his head to kiss her again. His yearning look made her pull away.

Don't worry, Mama. I won't forget.

"C'mon, let's get in," she said, taking his hand and jumping off the back of the boat feet first.

"Help me get on the tube!" she said, grabbing the ring as he bolstered her up and swam to the other one.

"Ready, Cece?"

"Ready!"

"Jake, hit it!"

With river water spraying her face, Cecilia gripped the handles of the tube as Jake dragged them behind the boat at full throttle. The rest of the day she spent on the boat drinking tequila to numb the constant pain in her heart.

"I need to get out of this wet suit and put on some dry clothes," she said with a shiver as the sun set.

"Grab your bag, and let's go."

Everyone else was in the cottage, passing the bong around when they got there.

"Save some for me," she said while throwing her bag over her shoulder and meandering down the long hall, steadying herself with a hand on each wall. "I'll be back in a minute."

No one looked up or said anything to her. A thick haze of smoke hung heavily in the air.

Closing the door to the tiny hall bathroom, she let out a hollow laugh and flicked the light switch repeatedly—on, off, on, off—allowing the darkness to overcome the light. She slid onto the bathroom floor, sitting in pitch blackness, a total eclipse of her soul.

"Hey, Cece, ya doing okay in there?" Chris asked as he gently tapped on the wooden bathroom door. "You've been in there a while."

"Yeah, I'll be out in a minute." Struggling out of the wet bathing suit, she dried off and stumbled to put her jeans and t-shirt on.

Chris was waiting for her when she opened the door. "I need to get you home. I didn't realize how late it was. What have you been doing in there?"

"Just thinking."

Without asking any questions, he grabbed her bag and headed to the truck.

Once he pulled into her driveway, Chris stared at the front door.

"I guess he scares you too." Cecilia knew Daddy had a reputation around town, and no one wanted to mess with him when he drank.

"He does, now hurry up and get out!" he nervously joked as he leaned over to kiss her.

Cecilia closed the truck door and went around back, hoping to sneak in and get to her room without stirring up any pandemonium.

The house was dark. She put her key in the lock and turned the knob as quietly as she could. Stepping in, she could hear heavy breathing.

"Daddy? Is that you?"

The door closed behind her.

He looped his arm around her neck, his other hand cupping her mouth. Cecilia elbowed him in the stomach, causing the hand sealing her mouth to loosen enough for her to bite his fingers as hard as she could. Daddy yelled a stream of cuss words as Mama came to the door and flipped the light switch on.

"What's going on here?" Mama shouted.

"Who told her she could go out?!"

"I did! Now leave her alone!" Mama turned to her and commanded, "Cecilia, get in your bedroom now!"

Cecilia did as she was told, locking herself in and quickly putting the chair against the door.

"Please, God, don't let him kill her!"

Morning came. Daddy left for work, and Cecilia could hear Mama talking on the phone to someone.

I guess I owe you a thank you, God. So, well, thanks. He didn't kill us.

With school starting soon, she left the house whenever she could get away from Daddy. She spent time at the beach with friends, drinking tequila or whatever was available to help her escape the haunting sound of the suction that played in her mind like a scratched record skipping at the same spot over and over again. *No one,* other than Josh, Ana, and Mama, knew her deep secret, and she would keep it in the dark.

It had been taken care of.

AHH, THE REVOLVING door. The step-in had changed everything. Cecilia had stepped out raw and emotionally detached. School started. Miss Personality and Homecoming Queen with trophy boyfriend at her side. Class president. Honor roll. The smile. The laugh. The confidence. All fake.

What would they think if they knew the truth, Cecilia?

The table. Stirrups. Suction canister. All showed up as uninvited guests when least expected to remind her of **that** day. The demons continued to war within her mind.

"CECILIA?"

"What, Mama?"

"Did you ask your daddy if you could go out tonight?"

"A few nights ago, he said it was alright!" Cecilia always had to catch Daddy at just the right time to ask permission to go on a date. Her odds of him saying yes were more favorable if he wasn't angry, shouting, or cursing about something.

"He seems to have forgotten and says you have to stay home."

"Mama, Chris is supposed to be here in about an hour."

"You better go talk to him then."

Cecilia closed her eyes and tried to stay calm. She knew she would have to intentionally craft her words if she had any chance of going out. Daddy was sitting in his chair, the television turned on full blast as usual.

"Da…ddy, is it okay if I turn the TV down for a minute?" she asked as she moved toward it.

"Whatcha want?"

"You said I could go to the movies with Chris tonight. I asked you on Wednesday and already told him you said it was all right."

Daddy started to get up, and Cecilia jumped back, afraid he would hit her.

"Did I?"

"Yes, Daddy. You did."

"Well, we have a lot of work to do tomorrow. I don't want ya to think you can sleep all morning."

She noticed Daddy trying to look around her to see his television show.

"I won't," Cecilia said, holding back the tears. "I planned to mow the grass and weed the flower beds."

"All right, but you better not be late comin' in."

"I won't, Daddy. I'll be home by eleven," she said, clutching her hands.

"Now turn the TV back up!"

"Yes, sir," she said before going to her bedroom.

"Sophia, why does he always do this to me before I go somewhere? My stomach hurts now! Maybe he'll pass out, and I'll be able to meet Chris outside. He didn't even make sense when Chris picked me up last time. I wish I could slam my door and scream and yell! I'm so sick of this. I can't wait to get out of this house! I have to beg for everything. Don't worry, girl," Cecilia said, looking at Sophia, "I'll take you with me."

By now, her tears were flowing. *So, God, is this what a father's all about? Someone who makes you beg and work to have fun? Someone who tells you one thing and then changes his mind? Someone who comes into your room at night and threatens you if you cry? And then he expects you* *to go to church on Sunday by yourself while he stays home and gets drunk? Well, **no, thank You, Father God!***

CECILIA HURRIED TO put on her new jeans and rodeo shirt. Forgetting about Daddy, she tightened her belt buckle and slipped her cowboy boots on. It was like stepping into another place and time. "It won't be long now, Texas!" she said, giving herself a final once over in the mirror. Cecilia had dreamed of the Texas rodeo and meeting a real cowboy since she was a little girl. Laughing, she kicked her boots off, trading them for her flip-flops tonight. "I might just need to get more sand between my toes before I go!" She rolled her sleeves up and went to check on Daddy.

Thank god he's asleep!

She saw Chris pulling into the driveway through the front window. "Mama, Chris is here. Is it okay if I go out the backdoor so he doesn't ring the bell and wake Daddy up?"

"Yes, go on and hurry out."

She was sure Mama didn't want him to wake up yet. It would allow her to work outside in the flowerbed before dark without him finding something to fight about. Her flower garden had become her sanctuary.

Chris had just gotten out of his truck when she came around the corner.

"Hey," she said as he opened the door for her. Cecilia reached for the handle, pulled herself up into the truck, and gave him a quick smile.

"You look nice," he said, grinning. "Are we still going to the movies?"

"How bout sunset on the beach?" she asked, relieved to be away from Daddy.

Closing her door and getting back in the truck, he reached under the seat, pulled out a bottle of vodka, and danced it right into her hands while maintaining his mischievous grin. He grabbed a cold beer from the cooler and popped the top.

"Isn't your daddy gonna miss his liquor?" she asked as she opened the bottle and took a swig, chasing it with his cold beer.

"No, he's got so much, he doesn't even know what he has! That is, as long as I don't take the last bottle of something. Let's get this truck on the beach now!" he said, taking the bottle and helping himself to a big gulp. Putting the truck into four-wheel drive, he entered the hard-packed sandy beach an hour before sunset.

As the salty breeze blew through the truck, she glanced at him and then back out her open window, mesmerized by the waves crashing on the shore. *I love it here…but will it always remind me of that night?* Turning back to Chris, she reached for the bottle.

Her fleeting thought disappeared with a new distraction. "Hey, stop! Look at that feeding frenzy!" Dozens of seagulls were skimming the water, devouring their catch, with the fittest getting their fill first. "Let's get out here!"

He stopped, and she jumped out of the truck, leaving her flip-flops on the floorboard. "Catch me if you can!" she teased, running toward the ocean.

"Oh, I will!" They ran up the beach, laughing and splashing each other with the cold ocean water until they finally collapsed in the sand. With her arms above her head, he rolled over beside her with his face touching hers. "I'm not sure how I'll make it without you!"

"Oh, you're probably gonna forget all about me. You know, out of sight, out of mind!"

"Seriously, I'm gonna miss ya, Cece! You make me laugh. I'm happy when I'm with you."

"This isn't going to be forever," she said, already knowing in her heart that it would be. "I'll be home as much as possible, and you can always visit me."

"I don't know, but I feel this is it for us, and I don't want what we have to end."

"Let's not think about tomorrow. Just hold me now," she said, leaning closer to kiss him.

12

THE DAY CECILIA had longed for finally arrived.

"Mama, if Daddy can't come sober, I don't want him at graduation."

"He'll be sober. I warned him the other morning before he left for work or had a chance to drink anything. I think it shocked him. He looked me in the eyes and said he hadn't planned on drinking anything. Josh and Ana will pick us up, and we'll all ride together."

Mama saw the worried look on her face.

"Don't worry. Josh won't let him in the car if he's drunk."

Cecilia sighed. She had heard his lies before.

Learning came quickly for her, and the golden honors tassel hanging over her cap proved it. Her drive and perseverance paid off with a full four-year scholarship to the University of Texas in Austin, her dream come true. As valedictorian of her class, she brought the crowd to their feet with an inspiring speech on how success was made of hard work and determination.

EVERYONE CHANGED CLOTHES back at the house. Cecilia saw Daddy unlock his shop and go in.

"Mama, where are you?"

"I'm in the kitchen with Josh and Ana."

"Mama, Daddy's in the shop. You know that's where he keeps his liquor. Can't he just go one day without drinking? I don't want any trouble today!"

"I'll go out there and hang with him," Josh said. "Maybe that'll slow him down a little."

"Cecilia, you and Ana help me get the table set and the tea poured," Mama said, ignoring her cry for help. "The food's almost ready." Mama had cooked most of it the day before and was warming up the spiral ham, green beans, and squash casserole. She had already put the homemade bread and butter pickles out and couldn't stop talking about the lemon meringue pie for dessert.

Mama peered through the kitchen window and saw Josh and Daddy under the oak tree. The anger Daddy displayed on his face and the flailing of his arms as he towered over Josh made Mama's skin bristle.

"Cecilia, go tell Josh and your Daddy the food is ready, and if they want it hot, they better come on in now."

"Hey, it's lunch time," Cecilia called from the door. "Mama said you need to come in."

Josh made his way to the house while Daddy followed behind with a scowl.

Daddy washed his hands and sat at the table's head. "Cecilia, you **say** the blessing. **You** go to church. Seems right since this is your last meal with us for god knows how long," he taunted.

She waited for everyone to sit down and promptly said the blessing before he could say anything else. She could sense he had more on his mind, which probably wasn't good.

"Lord, thank You for this food. Amen."

Mama began passing the food around. When everyone had their plates full, Josh tapped his fork on the side of his glass and waited to get their attention.

"Cecilia, I want to say how proud I am of you. You'll be the first one in our family to go to college. And it's all paid. Hear, hear! Good job! To Cecilia," he said, raising his glass in a toast.

Ana and Mama joined in. Daddy just kept eating.

"Thank you," she said, staring down at her plate, too afraid to say more.

"Why does she have to go across the country to a university?" Daddy interrupted. "What's wrong with her staying here and going to college? There's a campus down in Manteo. Is she too good for that? She could stay here and pay us rent while she goes to school. We've supported her all these years," he ranted as if she wasn't even in the room.

The room grew quiet. Cecilia jumped when the cubes fell from the ice maker.

"Why would you want that, Daddy? So you could have extra money for all your booze?" she asked, without thinking of the consequences.

Daddy stood up and drew his hand back to slap her face.

"No!" Mama screamed.

Josh quickly grabbed his hand and shoved him back down into his chair. Ana got up from the table, and the two left before Daddy could retaliate.

Mama didn't say a word. She started clearing the dishes and motioned for Cecilia to go to her room as Daddy spewed curse words.

Cecilia sat on the bed, covered her ears and rocked back and forth until the backdoor slammed and the shouting ceased.

It wasn't long before Mama knocked on her bedroom door.

"Cece, may I come in?"

She unlocked the door, and Mama came and sat beside her bed. "I'm sorry. I am." Mama pulled an envelope out of her apron and handed it to her. "I've been saving some money and want you to have it. I'm sorry it can't be more. Put it somewhere safe. You'll have it when you need it. I'm proud of you, Cecilia. I want you to make something of yourself. I want you to get as far away from here as you can. I only wish I had been brave like you."

"Mama, I'm not brave. I'm scared all the time. Why don't you leave him? You could go to Aunt Katherine's."

"No, I belong here. If I was going to leave, it should've been a long time ago. It's too late now."

"No, it's not!"

She placed her finger to Cecilia's lips. "Shhh. It's okay now. I'll be all right. Keep in touch and let me know how you're doing."

"I will, Mama."

13

CECILIA HAD STAYED up late packing the car while Daddy slept off his drunken stupor. The day's events and the thought of the long drive coming up, made it difficult for her to fall asleep, even though she was exhausted.

The smell of crisp bacon and coffee brewing drew Cecilia out of bed and to the kitchen table early the following day, where she found it set for two with Mama's rose china and good silver. There was no sign of Daddy. Cecilia jumped when she heard footsteps. Turning, she saw Mama with a basket of homemade biscuits and blueberry jam.

"Good morning. I thought we might have breakfast together before you leave. Take your plate and get some bacon and eggs from the stove. I'll pour you some coffee. The cream's on the table."

Once her plate had been fixed, she sat down beside Mama and slowly sipped her coffee.

"Mama, where's Daddy?"

"He's working in his shop today."

"Should I go out there and apologize?"

"I don't think so. I wouldn't want you to start your trip all upset."

"Yeah, you're probably right. This is good and tastes even better on this fancy china," Cecilia said, trying to make light of the heaviness that hovered over them. "Thanks for cooking."

"It's nothing. I'm sending you a cooler with some food from

yesterday. I put plenty of ice in there, so it should be good for a while," Mama said, trying not to choke up. "There's some drinks in there, too."

"Thank you."

"Well, we don't want all that good food to go to waste," she said as they finished eating in silence.

Mama got up to clear the table. "I doubt he'll come out to say goodbye."

Cecilia nodded. "It won't take me too long to get ready." *Am I supposed to eat breakfast on this fancy china and pretend like growing up in this family hasn't been a living hell? I better stop before this undertow of emotions pulls me into a dark place I don't want to go. Besides, I'm getting away. I wish Mama were getting away, too.*

"I see Josh pulling up now. He took your car, changed the oil, and had everything checked out for you."

"That's nice. I'll be out in a few minutes."

Cecilia went to her room for a final check to ensure she hadn't forgotten anything and to get Sophia. "Come on, girl! You didn't think I'd leave without you, did you?"

Mama and Josh stood by the car. Daddy was nowhere in sight. "Thanks, Josh, for taking care of my car! That means a lot!"

"I'd never send my favorite sister off with dirty oil!"

Forcing a smile, she reached up to hug him. "I'm your only sister, you nut."

"Take care of yourself," Mama said nervously, hoping she would leave before Daddy came out and tried to start something ugly.

With no sign of Daddy and Sophia wedged between a few small boxes on the front seat, Cecilia started the car and backed out of the driveway.

"Sophia, it's you and me now, girl!" she said, putting her sunglasses on and tuning the radio to the oldies station to hear the Eagles singing, "Life in the Fast Lane." Cecilia pressed the gas pedal to the floorboard and sped down the road. "Is this what freedom feels like, Sophia?" she asked with teary eyes. "Will I ever be free from the hurt in my heart, Soph? Why don't you grace me with a little of your wisdom?"

Cecilia hit start on the GPS. "Great, only 1,533 miles and

twenty-three plus hours to go, girl! I sure am glad you're gonna keep me company!"

What if he was right? Maybe I should have gone to school closer to them so I could make sure Mama was okay. Who do I think I am anyway?

THE DAY WAS growing dark, and the temperature was dropping as Cecilia entered the town of King's Mountain and saw the sign "Cabins for Rent." Signal on, she turned right and headed down the dirt road to the rental office. Outside stood a replica of the Liberty Bell. She gave it a big tug, which emitted a deep, bellowing sound. A sound that summoned the white-bearded man wearing blue jean bib overalls to open the door and emerge from his office.

"What can I do for ya, miss?" he asked.

"Do you have any cabins available for tonight?"

"Yes, ma'am," he said with a newfound excitement for a paying customer. "Come into the office, and I'll get ya a key while you sign in."

Cecilia reached into her wallet and thought of Mama as she pulled out some of the money she had given her.

"With tax, that'll be eighty-five dollars and ninety-eight cents," the old man said.

"Thank you, Mama," she said under her breath while handing the man a hundred dollar bill.

"Thank you, ma'am," he said as he counted back her change and handed her a receipt..

"It's at the top of the hill. One bedroom, fresh sheets, and a coffee pot plugged in and ready to go. There's a stack of dry firewood on the porch if you want to build a fire in the fireplace. Nights can still get a little chilly around these parts in May," he said.

"Thanks, I appreciate that."

"You bet. If you're hungry in the morning, there's some pretty good breakfast in the diner next door."

She took the key and made her way to the cabin. Yawning, she turned the key and opened the door to the smell of pine wood and the sight of a big bear's head hanging over the fireplace.

"Are you gonna be staring at me all night? Sophia will be keeping an eye on you! Speaking of Sophia, I better get her outta the car."

Grabbing Sophia and the cooler Mama had packed, Cecilia slung her backpack over her shoulder and took everything in before going back out to grab some firewood.

Gathering an armful, she placed it in the fireplace and stuffed some old newspaper under the grate. Striking the match, the paper blazed, lighting up the room. She opened the cooler, pulled out the ham and cheese sandwich Mama had made, and flopped on the couch. Looking at the sandwich reminded her of the graduation lunch that had gone awry. She squinted as she remembered Daddy's hand barely missing her face. "It was my fault! I knew better than to come back at him. I ruined lunch for everyone," she cried. "Mama, I'm sorry. Thank you for trying to make breakfast special this morning."

Putting the ham and cheese back in the cooler, she pulled out the lemon meringue pie. "I'd share with you, Sophia, but I know you don't eat sweets," she said between sobs. Lifting the fork to her mouth, she stopped crying and looked at Mama's pie. She wiped her eyes with her other hand and let the smooth lemon flavor caress her taste buds. "Mama, you *always* said that one bite of your lemon meringue pie would fix anything. Thank you. I hope you're alright tonight," she said aloud while texting her to let her know she was okay.

I DON'T WANT YOU WORRYING ABOUT ME. I MADE IT TO KING'S MOUNTAIN AND WILL GO TO BED AS SOON AS I SHOWER! LOVE YOU MAMA.

Cecilia glanced at the table and noticed Sophia's leaves were starting to droop. "Hey girl, how about I give you a little drink, and then I'll get a fast shower so we can get a good night's sleep before we hit the road again?"

Cecilia watered the plant and put it on the nightstand beside the bed.

"You think that's a wonderful idea."

"Good. I do, too. Let's just hope this storm moves around us. I sure am glad nobody can hear me talking to you! They'd think I was crazy for sure! We'll keep this between the two of us!"

Brushing her teeth while waiting for the shower water to warm, Cecilia thought of Daddy and how he always yelled if she ran too much water. "Well, Daddy, I'll run all the water I want to now! I'll show you. You *wouldn't* even come out to tell me goodbye! What kind of father are you?"

Cecilia stood under the shower head while the water washed her tears down the drain. "Forget you, Daddy!" she said as she stepped out of the shower, dried off, and quickly put on her pajama pants and UT t-shirt.

She opened the front door and ran out to make sure she had locked the car doors. The night air was still and quiet except for a few crickets chirping. In the distance, sheets of lightning flashed with a clap of thunder, applauding its performance now and then. "Keep your show over there," she said as a sudden gust of wind rushed across the porch. Closing the front door, she locked it and stoked the fire. It crackled as the last piece of log fell into the hot embers.

She thought of Mama as she turned back the bed covers. The patchwork quilt reminded her of all the ones Mama had made. Sliding under the sheets, she pulled the quilt up around her face. *There's no need to put a chair against the door tonight,* she thought as she turned over and closed her eyes.

By three AM the storm had found its way to the little rustic cabin. Cecilia stirred and woke to the sound of the screen door slamming as each gust of wind blew it open and snapped it shut. The rain pelted against the window panes, causing them to rattle.

"It's just a storm," she said, trying to calm herself.

Grabbing Sophia, she fumbled to the bathroom with her pillow and blanket. Locking the door, she crawled into the bathtub and placed Sophia on the rim.

"I'm not brave, Mama. I'm not! I'm not brave, Mama…"

ECILIA WOKE THE following day with a kink in her neck and a slight headache.

Grabbing the handicapped bar, she pulled herself up out of the tub. Putting on jeans and a clean sweatshirt, she gathered her belongings, packed the car, and headed up the dirt road toward the gas station and the diner. "Well, Soph, that ham sandwich doesn't seem too appealing this morning, but some blueberry pancakes and bacon might hit the spot."

An older gentleman stood by the diner door as if waiting for her.

"Good morning," he said as he smiled and opened the door.

"Thank you."

The man nodded his head. "The pleasure's all mine."

"Do I know you?"

The man just smiled again and walked toward the road.

"Just one?" the hostess asked.

"Yes," she answered while turning to look for the man.

"A booth or the counter?"

"A booth."

"Okay, take your pick; a waitress will be there in a minute."

"Thanks."

Cecilia looked out the window. The man was gone.

The waitress came, handed her a menu, and proceeded to ramble about the day's special: ham and eggs with pancakes and grits.

"That's fine. Please leave off the ham." *I don't think I'll ever eat ham again.* "Could I also get some coffee with cream and sugar and orange juice?"

"Sure thing."

Curious about the old photographs on the diner's wall, Cecilia moved closer. She studied the strangers' faces within each black-and-white portrait and found it odd that no one, not even the children, had a smile.

"What are *your* stories?" she whispered. "I remember the last time we had a family picture together." *Josh had a black eye Daddy had given him the night before, which Mama meticulously concealed with her foundation. It had been a hard night for me, too. I just didn't have a black eye to show for it. The photographer told us to smile, and we did as he said.*

The cook rang the bell for food pick up, and Cecilia returned to her booth. When the waitress brought the food, Cecilia noticed a tattoo on her left arm that read D 31:6 and a picture of a roaring lion's face sketched in bright colors.

"Hey, what's your tattoo about?"

"It's a scripture in the Bible from Deuteronomy 31:6 that says God will never leave you.

Sometimes I just need that reminder. God's always had my back, even when I didn't feel like He did. He's fought my battles and has done things for me I could never have done for myself."

"Glad it worked out for you. God's never done any of that for me. He must have been busy fighting *your* battles when *I* needed Him," she said sarcastically.

The waitress slid into the other side of the booth and reached for Cecilia's hand. "Hey, I'm sorry, but He's here and working things out even when we can't see or understand Him."

Cecilia pulled her hand away and stared at the waitress. "Well, I'll never understand it!"

"He loves you, girl. He didn't cause all those bad things in your life that must have left you so angry. We live in a world where evil and bad things happen, but He's always with us, and if we trust Him, He'll work it all out for our good." The waitress pulled her ticket and wrote her name and number on the back. "Here, I'm Mandy. If you ever need to talk, give me a call."

Chugging her orange juice, Cecilia threw some dollar bills down on the table, along with Mandy's number, and got up to leave.

"Aren't ya gonna eat your breakfast?"

"I just lost my appetite," Cecilia said while going to the door.

I will never leave you!! Right? Slamming the car door, she blasted the music, squealed her tires, and took off down the road.

"So you think I'm brave, Mama? Okay, I'll be brave for you, but not for God!"

15

"**O**KAY, ESTOY TERMINADA," Cecilia said as she turned off her Spanish lesson for the day. She just passed the "Welcome to Alabama" sign and could feel the fatigue. She pushed through as her destination was Jackson, Mississippi.

Sitting silently was not happening. Cecilia squirmed to stay awake. Her mind wandered into random thoughts of crashing her car at 70 mph or falling asleep and waking up in a hospital with amnesia or being paralyzed from the neck down.

"Cece, get it together."

Just then, a text message came in. It was Mama. YOU ALRIGHT? She took a deep breath and decided to call her.

"What's wrong?" Mama asked.

"No hello?"

"Oh, honey, I'm sorry; I'm just nervous about your long drive."

"Everything's fine. I'm in Alabama."

"That's a lot of driving."

"I know. I'm gonna find a place, get something to eat, and crash."

"Don't say crash."

"Mama, please, you know what I meant."

She could hear Mama sigh. "I know. Just be safe, okay?"

"I will."

"Josh is here. He wants to talk to you."

Cecilia could hear Josh's voice in the background.

"Hey, sis, so the car's running good? No problems?"

"No problems, thanks to you!"

"Everything else good?" he asked.

It seemed strange to Cecilia that his voice had a different inflection. Was she overreading things?

"Hey, Josh?" Cecilia was uncertain about what to say.

"Yes."

"Have you seen anyone?" she asked.

"Anyone? Like, am I dating someone?"

"No, you idiot. I mean, is anyone strange in the neighborhood?"

"Okay, you're freaking me out. Like a stalker?"

"Forget it."

"No, what is it?"

"It's nothing, just a bad dream I had the other night," she said, brushing off her peculiar question about seeing a stranger.

"Well, you know what Dad says about bad dreams," he said.

"Very funny. Hey, I've gotta go. I think I see a place to stay tonight."

"Okay, later."

"Tell Ana hello for me."

"You got it, sis."

Cecilia ended the call. *What was I thinking, asking Josh about strangers in the neighborhood? Did I think the guardian might still be there or was that the guardian that held the door for me at the diner? Is he following me?*

Hunger pulled her from those thoughts as a Texas Roadhouse right beside a Motel 6 came into view.

"It looks like they left the light on for us, Soph!" she laughed. "I'll call the food order in after we check in to the motel, and then I'll pick it up. What would you like?"

Cecilia stared at the plant on the seat beside her.

"Nothing? Come on now. It's been a long day! Okay, I know. I'm nagging. How about you come to the pool with me and sit on the table while I eat?"

She looked at Sophia like she expected her to answer.

Yes.

"Perfect! I thought you'd like that."

The pool area was empty except for two men sitting together at a corner table, drinking beers and talking.

Cecilia scanned the exits and sat facing them at the table closest to the door.

"Sophia, are they creepy-looking to you? Yeah, me too!" she said out loud while pretending to talk on her phone. "I think the one on the left is staring at us. Act like you don't notice."

Cecilia opened the takeout container and began eating her steak and fries.

"Sophia, maybe I'm just overreacting. You know we haven't slept much, and I've been driving all day. It's okay. I know you don't like to drive. You're still great company. Hey, they're getting up. Don't stare, but they're coming our way."

Cecilia jumped when the men threw their glass beer bottles in the trash at the same time, causing them to clang together loudly. They stood there and continued talking.

She gathered her trash, threw it away, grabbed Sophia, and headed back to the elevator. Turning around, they were so close, she bumped into them.

"Oh, sorry," she said, stepping to the side.

"It's our fault. Ladies first," the tall, skinny one said as he motioned for her to continue.

She stopped and pushed the elevator button. Holding Sophia close to her chest, she took a deep breath and entered when the door opened. The two men stepped in behind her.

The door opened to the second floor, and Cecilia stepped out. Behind her came the men.

With the key in her hand, she paused by her door to see if they were going by.

"It looks like you could use a little help," the tall, scruffy one said. "Your hands are pretty full."

And pretty sweaty, she thought as her racing heartbeat caused pain in her chest. "No, thank you." *What do I do?*

At about that time, a large family unloaded from the elevator and walked toward her.

"Mama, what took y'all so long? Will you help me?" Cecilia asked with a wide-eyed look.

The men smiled, walked down the hall, and turned the corner.

"Are you okay?" the woman holding the baby asked.

"Yes, ma'am. I felt uncomfortable when those men offered to help me open the door. I thought they would leave if my family were here. I'm sorry."

"Well, you might want to let the desk clerk know."

"I'll do that. Thank you."

Cecilia's hand shook as she put the card in the slot to open the door. After quickly utilizing all the lock options, she put Sophia on the table next to the bed.

"Girl, maybe I'm just paranoid," she said as she put the desk chair in front of the door. *Will I always need to barricade the door so I can sleep?*

The next day, she woke to people talking in the hall.

"Ten-thirty!" she groaned while scrunching her face up. "We've missed it, Soph!!! I dreamed I made the perfect waffle and loaded it with butter and maple syrup! Of all the days to sleep late! Now it's over! No free hotel breakfast for us!" She quickly got up, washed her face, and brushed her teeth. She threw everything into her backpack and headed to the car after grabbing a breakfast sandwich from the vending machine. "Soph, it looks like they didn't offer free breakfast anyway! I shouldn't have gotten so upset! Well, at least there's no sign of the strangers from the pool," she said while surveying the parking lot. "Today's gonna be a big day, Soph. By the end of the day, the great state of Texas should be welcoming us home! UT, here we come!!!"

HOUR AFTER HOUR, she pressed on with determination to reach her new destination.

"Soph, look for the 'Welcome to Texas' sign. It's coming up! Alright now, get ready, girl! Here we go! Woohoo," she yelled as all four wheels crossed the Texas state line. "Let's go be welcomed at the Texas visitor center, shall we?"

She pulled in and parked the car. "Sophia, I'll be right back to tell ya everything. We made it! I could just fall down and kiss the ground! But I won't. I know how embarrassed you'd be!"

Cecilia stood in front of the "Welcome to Texas" sign and took a selfie. "I can't wait to send this to Josh and Mama." Looking at the picture, she froze with the hair on her arms and the nape of her neck standing at attention. She looked behind her but saw no one. Trembling, she enlarged the picture to see the form of a tall, slender man blurred in the background.

Is that him? The man who opened the door for me at the restaurant? The one who took my hand and helped me up the steps that night? The one who sat with me at the hospital? The one who paid my bill? Is he following me? Wanting to run and hide, she darted into the bathroom and splashed cold water on her face. She pulled out her phone to look at the picture again and cringed to see the mysterious figure had disappeared.

"Um, uh, am I seeing things now?" Trembling, she wiped the sweat from her face and locked herself in the bathroom stall. She closed her eyes and took a deep breath.

"Ouch," she cried, realizing she had bitten her lip. Touching her mouth with some toilet tissue, she saw blood and felt weak. Thoughts of the procedure and the restaurant where blood had filled the toilet ran rampant as she threw the paper in and flushed.

I just want to go home. No, I never want to go home!

Unlocking the stall, she hurriedly washed her hands, splashed some more water on her face, put some pressure on her lip with her hand, and quickly darted to the car.

"Soph, I must be delirious. I'm seeing things. The whole guardian thing is making me crazy. And for god's sake, I'm talking to a plant!!!"

The conversations in her head continued, though, leaving little reprieve and soon became unbearable to the point she pulled over at a rest stop. The battle raged, a relentless fight for her self-worth and identity. *You can't do this. You **do** need to go home. You're afraid of your own shadow,* the voice mocked. Cecilia walked up and down the sidewalk, trying to regain her composure and eliminate the sour taste in her mouth.

"How long am I gonna keep listening to these lies?!" Her breathing became easy. She had a new sense that everything was going to be okay. "No! Enough is enough!" she said, returning to the car. "I was valedictorian of my class! And *I did* that! All on my own! And I can do this!" she yelled while getting in and slamming the door.

"Let's go, Soph!" she said, opening the window. "Fresh air! That's what we need, girl!"

16

DETERMINED TO GET there as soon as possible, Cecilia drove for the next four and a half hours with just one bathroom stop.

"Soph, can you feel that? The temperature's dropping," she said while rolling her window up. "This isn't looking too good." The sun was setting, and dark clouds painted the sky gloomy as the dismal weather threatened a storm. Cecilia gripped the steering wheel with every forceful gust of wind to prevent the car from swerving over the middle line into the other lane. Heavy drops of rain pummeled her windshield as the monstrous clouds burst open. Sitting up straight and leaning forward, she strained to see the road. As if the road conditions weren't enough, her cell phone service dropped, and so did her stomach. Cecilia panicked as she fumbled with her phone to get her GPS back. Another buffeting wind hit the car, causing her to grab the wheel with both hands. Her GPS came back on, but it was too late; she had missed her turn-off.

"Is this what the road to eternal damnation feels like? Pitch black and never-ending? Where are the cars? Am I the only one out here on this god-forsaken road?" She felt her spine tingle like an alarm buzzing with impending doom. "Focus, Cecilia! Just focus! We're on the home stretch! We can do this. Oh no!" she cried. The car began to slow down and sputter as she approached the railroad track. "No!!! Are you kidding me? Sophie, we're on empty!"

The Toyota sputtered while only its front wheels made it over the track. "Oh, my god!" Cecilia screamed as the red, blinking light pierced the darkness in tune with the roar of the freight train pounding the rails. "Help me, God!" she yelled, putting the car in neutral and pushing it over the tracks. She dared not look down the track for fear of becoming paralyzed as she heard the rumbling sound of the approaching train. Continuing to push, the Toyota made its way off the track and onto the side of the road. Heart pounding, she turned around just in time to see *him* on the other side of the track before the train clamored by, obstructing her view. "Who are you?" she screamed, but her words were lost in the squeal of the train wheels. By the time it had passed, he was gone, and the red light that had lit his face was now green. Frantically, she opened the car door and slid in. Locking the doors, she grabbed a sweater from the back seat and tried to calm herself.

"I could've been killed on that track!"

With her phone now dead, she reached for Sophie and stared into the night until she couldn't keep her eyelids open.

I will never leave you played over and over in her head as she drifted off.

CECILIA STIRRED THE following day as a young man tapped on her window. "Miss, are you alright?"

She opened the door as the man stepped back. "I'm outta gas."

"Have you been here all night?"

"Yes."

"Sure you're okay?"

"I think so. I'm still here."

She looked back to see a pickup truck towing a trailer with a lawn mower.

"I have enough gas in my gas can to get you to a nearby station."

"Thanks. That would be so nice of you."

She watched from her rearview mirror as he returned to his truck and brought the gas can back. He took the lid off her tank and began to pour it in.

"Okay, you should be set now."

"How much do I owe you?"

"Nothing," he said with a smile and returned to his truck.

"Thank you!"

"Welcome to Texas," he said while holding one hand up.

With relief, Cecilia started the car and was on her way again. Her phone finally lit up after getting enough of a charge. "Things are looking up, Soph! Here comes GPS! Are you ready to determine how far we are from our final destination?

Yes???

"Okay, here it is! We are one hour and fifteen minutes away!"

Stopping at the nearest gas station, she filled the tank and checked her text messages, noticing that Mama had sent eight. "Soph, I better text her now before we get back on the road. No, I need to hear her voice." Cecilia dialed Mama's cell phone but got no answer. *Maybe she's in the kitchen.* Cecilia dialed the house phone, hoping Mama would answer.

"Hello," Daddy said.

"Hello," he said again in an aggravated kind of way. "Who's this?"

"It's Cecilia."

"Well, well. I bet you were hoping to get someone other than me. Whatta ya want? Money? Are you calling for money? It's not so easy out there all by yourself, is it Cecilia? Maybe you should just turn around and get back where you belong!"

She could hear Mama asking for the phone. Click. The line went dead.

"Mama?!!" Cecilia cried as she began to text her. ARE YOU ALRIGHT? I'M SORRY FOR CALLING. I HOPE HE DIDN'T HURT YOU. PLEASE GO TO AUNT KATHERINE'S. YOU'LL BE SAFE THERE. I'M ALMOST TO AUSTIN.

Cecilia saw a text coming through from Mama: I WAS WORRIED ABOUT YOU. I'M OKAY. HE'S ALREADY BACK IN HIS CHAIR WITH THE TV BLARING. I'M GLAD YOU'RE GETTING

THERE SAFELY. I LOVE YOU. DON'T WAIT SO LONG NEXT TIME.

I WON'T. I LOVE YOU, MAMA.

I'm arriving alive, Mama. That's about all I can say.

17

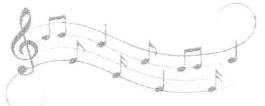

The phone call was like salt being rubbed into her wounds: "I'll show you, Daddy! I won't ever ask you for anything. I'd rather live on the streets than take anything from you. You want it to be hard for me, so I'll come back. I'll never go back to where you are, Daddy! Nobody's gonna hurt me again. I won't let them!!"

She took a deep breath and glanced over at her potted plant.

"Soph, sometimes you just have to cut yourself off from people. Let's listen to some music until we get there. I need to calm down, girl. My head is pounding. One more hour, and we'll be home!" Grabbing the bottle of Tylenol from her purse, she popped the top and swallowed two pills. "Two Tylenol may suffice for the pain in my head but I'm not sure what will ever stop this ache in my heart, Soph."

"There it is. Our new home." A wave of panic gained momentum as Cecilia pulled into the student parking lot.

"I can't go in. I can't do this." She blew out short breaths to gain control. "I've come all this way, and now I can't go in. I'm scared, Sophie."

With the battle beginning to rage again, she opened the car door and stepped out. *What are you doing here, Cecilia? Do you think you can do this? So, you think you're going to become a lawyer? Do you think you can defend someone? You can't even defend yourself. You're kidding yourself, Cecilia. Go home.*

"Shut up," she whispered. "I can do this. I've come too far not to."

She closed her eyes and took in a deep breath. *Just put your invisible mask on, Cecilia. You're so good at that.*

EVEN THOUGH IT was late afternoon, seniors still waited to sign in first-year students and direct them to their proper destinations. Cecilia stepped up to the table with Sophia in hand.

"Hi, welcome! I'm Abby. What's your name?" asked the slender brunette.

"Cecilia Evans."

"What kind of plant is that? It's different."

"I call it my angel plant. Not sure what its real name is."

"Well, it's gorgeous! I've never seen one like it."

"Thanks."

"You can sign in right here by your name and take your packet. You're on the second floor of the Kenner dorm, and your roommate's name is Jody Hines. She checked in earlier today. If you need anything, there's a resident advisor on your floor. Your class schedule is in the packet."

"Thanks, Abby," she said while thumbing through the packet and walking toward the dorm.

"Well, that wasn't so hard, Soph!"

When she got to her room, the door was slightly ajar. "Anybody here?"

"Be out in just a minute," came a response from the bathroom.

Cecilia glanced around the room. On the bed was a piece of wooden art with the Scripture *"Deuteronomy 31:6: I will never leave you nor forsake you."*

Really? She jumped when the door opened.

"Oh, sorry. I didn't mean to scare you. I'm Jody."

"I guess we're roommates then. I'm Cecilia, and this is my plant, which you may hear me refer to as Sophia sometimes. Don't worry," she said when she saw Jody's bewildered look. "I'm not crazy. We've just traveled a long way together."

"Then don't you worry! My car's name is Jack, and I always talk to him. Jack, you better start or else!" she laughed. "I put my stuff on this bed if that's okay with you," Jody said.

"Yeah, sure, I like the window." Cecilia went to the window sill and placed Sophia in her new home. As the sun highlighted her blossoms, Cecilia admired her breathtaking beauty. *Abby saw how unique and exquisite you are. I think we're gonna like it here just fine, girl.*

"Are ya hungry?" Jody asked, interrupting her thoughts.

"A little."

"Well, I'm starving. Do you want to grab something to eat and then come back and I'll help you unpack?" Jody asked while she carefully studied Cecilia.

"Yeah, sure."

"I know this great Thai restaurant on the drag I found when my parents and I came for orientation. How does that sound?"

Cecilia nodded yes. She had never made it to orientation. *It must be nice to have parents who can stay sober long enough to do things like orientation.*

Eating outside on the restaurant's patio was lovely. Cecilia picked at her food while she listened intently as Jody shared about breaking up with her high school boyfriend before moving to Austin.

"We were both going in different directions," she said. "He was going down a dead-end street, and I had to decide if I wanted to follow him there. He was happy working in the family business and never leaving Johnson City, North Carolina."

"Wow, two Tarheel girls ending up in Texas together. What are the odds of that? I'm from the Outer Banks of North Carolina," Cecilia added.

"It *is* strange, I guess, but here we are! It must be serendipity or something! Anyway, I was suffocating just thinking about never crossing the county line. The last I heard, he had already settled down with Darla, and they were planning a Christmas wedding. He didn't waste any time moving on. Someone said they heard she was pregnant.

I have big dreams, and I want a career. I want to make a difference in this world. I wanna see justice done. I don't want anyone telling me what to do or where and when I can go somewhere. I never want to depend on anyone!"

Cecilia's eyes locked with Jody's. *Maybe they had more things in common than she realized.*

"Depending on others gives them too much control over your life. I don't wanna depend on anyone either, *but* people will depend on *me* as their lawyer," Cecilia chimed in.

"Exactly!" Jody said and grabbed the bill. "I picked, I pay. Next time, you pick, and you can pay."

Cecilia, too tired to fight, politely said, "Thank you, but it will most likely be Raman noodles."

"I love Raman noodles. We can stay in and study together. I'm gonna need all the help I can get."

"Okay, it's a deal."

18

School started, and Jody continued to talk about her past. Cecilia was relieved Jody wanted to share so much about *herself*. That way, she didn't have to. Cecilia had placed a deadbolt on the door to her past and buried the key. Keeping busy with classes helped her to do just that. Her *Daddy* wounds were beginning to heal, yet they would still fester sometimes at night when it was dark and quiet.

"Hey, it's Saturday! Let's do something fun! My brain needs a mini vacation, even for only a few hours. Let's go float the river," Jody pleaded.

Cecilia hesitated but knew she didn't stand a chance. Jody would keep nagging and whining until she said yes. She rarely said yes to anything fun. *Her* outings were going to class, the library, and the cafeteria.

"Fine. Let's go," Cecilia said, finally relenting.

The girls raced down to the river and jumped in.

"Good call," Cecilia said as she lay back in her inner tube and splashed her feet in the brisk water. The sun warmed her soul. *If only I could stay here floating in the river, with all my cares rushing downstream.*

One moment in time, she thought, trying to hold on to something enjoyable.

Hours passed.

"Jody, I feel like a shriveled-up prune. I'm gonna go read for a while."

"That's fine. Just let me know when you're ready to go."

Jody stayed in the river talking to other tubers. She had no trouble meeting people with her extroverted personality.

Cecilia sat on the bank and pulled a book out of her backpack.

"Oh, my god! What *is* going on? Who's laying on their car horn and slamming the doors?" She turned just in time to see *his* face as he approached her. He was crazed-looking and shouting curse words. Cecilia froze, paralyzed by fear.

I've been looking for you. Did you think you could escape?

Cecilia let out a bloodcurdling scream. This monster of fear seemed to follow her everywhere. No escape. She squeezed her eyes shut and only opened them when Jody called her name, to find no one there.

Will I ever be free?

Exhausted and limp, Cecilia sat on the bank with a blank stare.

"Here, let me put this towel around you." Cecilia's body was cool to touch, her face pale, and her lips blue by the time Jody reached her.

"It's gonna be okay," Jody said as she pulled Cecilia close. "Please say something. Talk to me! You're scaring me!"

"Take me home."

Back in the dorm, Jody fixed some tea for her and sat on the floor while Cecilia sat on the couch. It was quiet until Cecilia broke the silence. "I'm sorry I scared you. Sometimes I'm afraid that someone is after me, and now and then, they *show up.*"

"I know that fear. May I tell you something?"

Cecilia nodded, knowing Jody would tell her even if she didn't want her to.

"In my senior year, some friends asked me to go to a party at Mindy's parents' lake house. Someone must have put something in my drink that night because everything became blurry, and everyone appeared to be moving in slow motion. I went to the back bedroom to lie down. My tongue felt thick, and voices were so slurred I couldn't understand what anyone was saying. I couldn't recognize faces, but I think someone locked the door, and then they…" Jody began to cry. "I couldn't scream because someone had their hand over my mouth. They hurt me, Cece. They really hurt me. I must have passed out."

Cecilia began to breathe fast and went to the window sill for Sophia. Clutching her close to her chest, she sat back down as Jody continued.

"Some deep fog had covered my brain, and the next thing I remember was waking up in the dark on the front steps of my house. Somehow, I made it in and woke up hours later with a crushing headache. I was too embarrassed to tell anyone. A month later, my period didn't come. I took a home test and found out I was pregnant. I hadn't been with anyone since that party. I was terrified. I knew it would embarrass my parents and cause them a lot of pain. I didn't tell anyone, but after I turned eighteen, I went to a clinic and had an abortion. I felt like the sooner I took care of *it*, the sooner I could move on. I didn't even know who the father was. I knew I had to do something about it quickly before it was too late."

"Sorry, Jody. I need to go to the bathroom."

"Your face is flushed. Are you okay?"

"I'm fine, really," she said, holding her hand up to stop Jody from saying anything more. "I'll be right back."

Cecilia stared in the bathroom mirror. *It was just tissue, right? Abortion? Why was she telling me about this?* By now, she had forgotten all about the river incident. She flushed the toilet and returned to the couch, hoping Jody would take a break, but she continued where she left off.

"Every time I walked down the street and saw a carload of guys ride by, I wondered who had done this to me. I'm sure whoever was involved that night was still having fun recounting their good time. I decided then that I would make it. I'd get a good education and become a lawyer. I wanted someone to suffer for their crimes like I suffered and still do. Every time I see a baby, it reminds me of the one I aborted. I feel God's gonna punish me by never allowing me to have children."

Jody noticed the blank stare on Cecilia's face. "I'm sorry for dumping all this on you, especially when you're dealing with something yourself.

It's just that my baby had a heartbeat. I saw it on the sonogram before the abortion, and I did nothing to stop them," Jody sobbed. "I've never been able to tell anyone what I did, and I think about it all the time."

Cecilia sat there transfixed as her mind wandered back to the night on the beach and the pain that followed her abortion.

"Cecilia?"

Shaking her head, tears rolled down her cheeks. "I am so sorry. It must have been horrible."

"It was."

"Jody… you're not alone. In high school, I had sex with an older guy I had just met at a party. It wasn't horrific, like what happened to you, but the results were the same. I quickly learned he had a girlfriend and couldn't care less about me. Eight weeks later, I still hadn't started my period, and guess what? I was pregnant and scared to death. I knew my dad would have killed me. My brother took me for an abortion. The abortion clinic told me it was only tissue, but I knew better in my heart. I didn't want anyone to know. I was so ashamed. I'm still ashamed."

"Thanks for telling me, Cece. I didn't know and I'm really sorry. Being able to share this with you, knowing you've gone through the same thing, helps me feel better for some reason."

Cecilia put Sophia back down and went over to hug Jody. "We'll get through this together."

"Together," they cried.

At that moment, the common thread of their pain and shame had knitted their hearts as one.

"Hey Cece, friends, forever?"

"Friends, forever."

19

3 ½ years later

CECILIA STAYED IN touch with Mama during college but never returned to North Carolina except to spend Christmas one year with Jody's family. Zilker Park became her favorite hangout, and she and Jody spent lots of fun time there listening to concerts. She had started a movie club, and the Paramount was their choice theater, with *Casablanca* at the top of their movie list. Chris had called a few times, but Cecilia wasn't interested in a relationship with anyone. This was her last semester of college, and she wanted to graduate at the top of her class. She had made that clear to Jody and everyone around her.

"ART THERAPY?!" CECILIA sighed. Their advisor had recommended it for anyone enrolled in psychology classes, which they both were.

"It's gonna be an easy A!" Jody insisted. "Don't sweat it. And it's on a Saturday so you won't have to worry about all your other classes. It'll be fun!"

Cecilia looked at Jody and burst out laughing. "Really? An easy A, huh? I can't even draw a stickman. We *shall* see. If art therapy lowers my GPA, I'll never forgive you, Jody Hines!"

"Oh, you of little faith," Jody said, beaming. "You've got this."

Saturday came, and the weather was beautiful.

"Let's ride our bikes to class."

"Okay, let's do it!"

They locked them to the rack outside the allied health building and made their way to the classroom with the sign outside that read *Art Therapy*.

They went in and found a seat by the window. The teacher had opened all the windows, allowing a cool breeze to filter through the classroom.

"Who is *that*?" Jody asked. "Aren't you glad you signed up now?"

A tall, muscular young man with brown eyes and jet-black hair stood at the front of the class.

"Hello everyone, my name is Judd Taylor. Welcome to art therapy. I started teaching here three years ago after I graduated with a master's in counseling. I'm also a licensed art therapist and do art therapy at a nearby psychiatric hospital every other week. How many of you know anything about art therapy?" A few hands went up. "Okay. How many of you registered for this class thinking it would just be an easy A?" Jody grinned at Cecilia. The rest of the class chuckled.

"It doesn't matter how you got here or why; I'm glad each of you found your way. I hope to make the class interesting enough that you might find a way to use the information learned here in whatever career path you choose."

Mr. Taylor sat on the edge of his desk. "Art therapy originated in 1942 when the British artist Adrian Hill developed the term after discovering the therapeutic benefits of drawing and painting while recovering from tuberculosis in a sanatorium. Art therapy has helped treat people suffering from post-traumatic stress syndrome, better known as PTSD, which can affect people in different ways, but one thing is for sure: it *is* real," he added emphatically. "Art therapy has been used with cancer patients, prisoners, and those dealing with substance abuse, to name a few."

Cecilia looked at Jody and started to get up, but Jody quickly reached for her hand, and with pleading eyes, she sat back down.

"Okay."

"Today, I want you to think outside the box," the professor said.

Great, Cecilia thought. *I like staying inside my box.*

Judd handed out sketch paper. "Close your eyes and think about the first picture that pops into your mind. Then, pick up your pencils and start sketching anything that reminds you of that picture," he instructed.

Cecilia immediately thought of Sophia and began to draw. She had never seen a plant like her. *Why do you make me feel so peaceful? Is it your brillant color, or that the guardian had cared enough to give you to me without asking anything in return?* Engrossed in her thoughts, she jumped when Jody whispered, "Let's go."

Grabbing her bag, she heard the teacher telling everyone to take their picture, elaborate upon it during the week, and bring it back to class next time. Cecilia noticed that Jody's paper was blank. Cecilia remained quiet, knowing that whatever needed to go on paper could not be forced.

Outside by their bikes, Jody said, "I think this was a bad idea. This class isn't what I thought art therapy was all about! I started thinking about Mindy's party and the river when you flipped out. Do we want to go back and revisit those times?"

"This class is about giving you some ways to manage those *times.* Let's give it a try. It was only the first class."

CECILIA WENT THROUGH the week of studying and exams, but her mind wandered back to art class. *Was it the art or the teacher? Or both? His voice was calming, and it sure didn't hurt that he was drop-dead gorgeous.*

THE FOLLOWING SATURDAY morning, Cecilia got up early to jog before class. When she got back to the dorm, Jody was still asleep.

"Hey, Jody, time to get up," she whispered while nudging her on the shoulder. "Remember we have art therapy class today?"

Jody rolled over and covered her head with the blanket. "I'm going to sleep in today."

"Are you sick? You never sleep in," Cecilia probed.

"I'm not sick, but I'm going to sleep in!"

"OK. I'll catch you later." Cecilia closed the door quietly and hopped on her bike.

Judd was at the door greeting everyone as she arrived. Feeling awkward, Cecilia said, "Hello," and took her seat. It felt strange being there without Jody. *After all, it was her idea.*

"Today," Judd began, "if anyone wants to expound on their picture from last week, feel free. Start with telling us who you are and what your major is."

Several people shared, but Cecilia decided to stay seated until *he* walked by her desk and stopped. Her heart beat faster, hoping he wouldn't call her out. *It was voluntary, right?*

Judd glanced down at her picture and then at her.

Cecilia's eyes locked onto the gold cross necklace he wore around his neck.

"That's nice," he said. "Would you like to say a few words about your art?"

"Sure," she said and made her way to the front of the class. *Great, Cecilia. I thought you would let everyone else talk, but one word from him, and you jumped!*

"My name is Cecilia Evans, and my major is Business with a minor in Psychology. I plan to attend law school here after graduation." Cecilia held up the picture of her flower. As she looked around the room, she thought it had to be much easier to share the most intimate details of someone else's life in a courtroom packed with strangers than anything personal about *herself* in this small classroom.

Cecilia looked to the back of the room, focused on the big round clock, and began to speak. "This is a picture of a plant someone gave me during a hard time. I felt a lot of peace when I started drawing it last week. The person who gave me this flower was someone I didn't know. For some reason, he seemed to care what was happening in my life and left it for me with no strings attached. He said it was for my garden. I suppose it represents hope because I *would* like to have a garden one day. Anyway, it brought me peace," Cecilia said with misty eyes.

Everyone began to clap, causing her eyes to shift from the clock to her classmates. Jody was in the back. She had been so focused she never saw her come in. Cecilia took her seat, wondering how much Jody had heard.

"Thank you for sharing, Cecilia," Judd said. "Would anyone else like to share?"

Jody raised her hand.

"Come on up," he said.

Jody went to the front of the class and held up her blank paper. "I'm Jody Hines. My major is Business with a minor in Psychology. I'll be attending law school after graduation at UNC in Chapel Hill, North Carolina," she said as she held up her paper. "Yep, this is my picture—a blank page. I almost didn't come today, but since I'm the one who dragged my friend here, I felt I owed it to her to show up. When I close my eyes, the pictures aren't pretty. So, for now, this is *my* picture. I hope I'll eventually be able to pick up a brush, but for now, I guess the first step was to pick up the paper."

Judd began to clap, and others followed.

Looking down, Jody hurried to take her seat.

"Jody, thank you. That took courage. I'm glad you felt safe enough to share with us," Judd said.

Cecilia stood and hugged Jody before she could sit down. "Thanks, Jody."

"Thank you, Cecilia."

"Art can be a beautiful expression of oneself or a way of expressing something that needs to be said when somebody cannot put their feelings into words. Sometimes, it's easier to express the emotion or pain or a part of the story on paper without speaking. Remember, behind every piece of art is a unique and real artist," Judd continued. "Your assignment for next week is to spend some time researching an artist and finding out about their life and how their art has touched others or them personally. If anyone is free on Thursday afternoon at three o'clock, we could go to the art museum downtown as a group and study the different kinds of art. I will leave a sign-up sheet at the front desk. Stop on your way out and sign it if you're available and would like to go."

Cecilia and Jody looked at each other and headed for the door. Both girls signed up for the field trip right away.

Judd's arm brushed against Cecilia's shoulder as she was leaving. She turned instantly to find him staring at her. His dark eyes had a depth and intensity that drew her in. For a moment, she realized she was in danger of falling into a deep well she might not be able to get out of.

"Cecilia, keep working on that picture. Art has a way of evolving as you continue painting."

Cecilia shook her head to acknowledge him and headed out the door. *Evolving, what does that mean?*

No. No. No. No. No. No, Cecilia thought. *NO! Period.*

Cecilia slammed the door to her heart and quickly attached the lock. She hoped Jody had not picked up on that *brief exchange of something* that had caused her heart to flip-flop.

When they returned to the dorm, Cecilia tried to keep the conversation focused on Jody, but that didn't work this time.

"Did you see the way Judd looked at you?" Jody asked.

"What are you talking about? I didn't see any such thing."

"Cecilia, I did, and I also saw you. You were mush! I've never seen you like that before. Admit it!" Jody laughed. "And I heard him talking about starting college right after high school, which makes him about twenty-six to twenty-eight years old."

Cecilia didn't join in with her laughter or find it amusing. "Whatever Jody. I'm not interested, but more importantly, he's my professor! I told you when we first met I'm here for one thing. To graduate and get into law school. I *will* be a lawyer. And not just any lawyer. I'll be one of the best and most sought-after. People will come to me because I'll have the reputation of winning the most difficult cases," she said passionately.

"I'm so glad you said *one* of the best since I'm right here with you."

Cecilia cracked a smile. "Okay, we'll be the two best lawyers out there. Case closed."

20

THURSDAY ARRIVED. CECILIA and Jody met the class at the art museum. Cecilia decided to keep her distance from Judd. If Jody had picked up on something, she sure didn't want *him* to.

Cecilia was fascinated by the artwork, especially the abstracts. She liked that she could interpret them herself. Several pieces caught her attention, and she lingered, so engrossed in the paintings that she didn't hear Judd come up behind her.

"Captivated by this grouping?"

Startled by the sound of his voice, she turned and touched his hand.

Too close, Cecilia. Step back. Keep that door closed.

"I didn't mean to scare you. I'll have to give a better warning when I come around," he said, smiling.

Cecilia couldn't help but notice the sparkle in his eyes, and something about the touch of his hands had caused the hair on her arms to stand up.

"I'm attracted to this painting, in particular," Cecilia said, returning her focus back to the artwork.

"Oh. What do you like about it?"

"It's deep with many layers, mysterious, and different. I believe I can feel the emotions of the artist. Is that normal?" she asked, blushing.

"Perfectly normal. What were your emotions when you studied this piece?"

"I felt pain and sadness but also a glimmer of hope," she said, keeping her eyes glued to the piece.

"I like the way you think, Cecilia Evans. Keep looking," he said as he walked to another student.

Jody gripped her arm and grinned. "Deep? Mysterious? Lots of layers? You're becoming the teacher's pet fast," she said in jest.

"Ha ha. Let's go. No, wait, I need to get the artist's name. I'll use this one for the assignment. RJM. Let's stop at the desk and see if they have any info."

"How may I help you ladies?" the clerk behind the counter asked.

"Do you have any information on the artists that display their work?" Cecilia inquired.

"Any piece in particular?"

"It's an abstract featured in the humanitarian section. The artist signed it RJM."

"I do. We are showcasing a group of artists who are donating their pieces to help raise funds for different charities. He has an interesting story. Here's his card," she said, handing it to Cecilia.

She took the card and quickly headed outside with Jody to sit on the bench. Cecilia began to read the card out loud. "Raymond Jesus Martinez. Death Row Inmate for Capital Murder. Texas State Penitentiary." Flipping the card over, she continued to read. "Proceeds from any artwork sale go to men or women needing drug addiction rehabilitation that cannot afford to pay."

Cecilia pressed her lips together tightly as her eyes widened.

"What's wrong?"

"Nothing."

"It's not nothing. What's up?"

"I'm just wrestling with something. Do you mind if I walk back to the dorm by myself? I need to think."

"Okay, sure, if that's what you want. I'll see you back there. You sure?" Jody asked again.

"Yes, I'll be fine."

Jody squeezed her arm. "Call if you need me?"

"I'll be fine!"

Cecilia's thoughts were spinning out of control. *RJM, you're just like the rest of them. Do you think you can make what you did okay by painting for charity?*

She turned around and ran back up the steps to the museum. Scanning the area for cameras and seeing none, she realized RJM's art was in an unsecured part of the museum. "You don't deserve to have your art hanging here! Besides, they don't even care if anyone steals it, RJM!" It was near closing time, and no one was around. She moved closer to the painting as if coming face-to-face with RJM himself. "How long are they gonna keep you on death row? What are they waiting for?! When are you going to get what's coming to you?!! Well, there's no hope for you, so don't think your artwork will get you out of there somehow!! I hate you, RJM!"

She grabbed his piece off the stand, darted into the bathroom, and threw it in the trash. "Just like you, RJM. Trash. Trash. Do you hear me? Trash!!!" she cried. All those years of her own abuse that went unpunished hounded her. She splashed water on her face and dried it on her shirt sleeve. *I have to get outta here.*

She felt the fire in her cheeks as she rounded the corner to go out. The lady at the desk was in the back room, shuffling papers. Cecilia calmly made her way out the door. Outside, she began to tremble in the night air. *What just happened? Am I crazy? If someone saw me, I could kiss a career in law goodbye!* Her stomach began to churn. *Too late now,* she thought, as she slowly put one foot in front of the other and made her way down the rest of the steps.

Back at the dorm, her hands shook, trying to unlock the door.

Jody opened it before she could turn the key.

"Cecilia? Everything alright?"

"Not really. I snapped when I found out that RJM was on death row for murder, and they were allowing his artwork to be on display for all to see. I got so angry. I don't know why. I'm fine now. Really. I just needed some fresh air. This week's been too much. I need to take a hot shower and get to bed early tonight."

Jody began to say something, but Cecilia quickly cut her off. "I don't wanna talk about it."

That night, Cecilia moaned louder and louder as she tossed and turned in bed. A loud gunshot rang out, and she felt the pain of the bullet, yet it was RJM's victim who dropped to the ground, spewing blood everywhere. The blood was splashing up into Cecilia's eyes. She kept trying to wipe the blood from her eyes so she could get a better glimpse of the man calling her name. She opened her eyes and found Jody hovering over her, crying.

"Cece, talk to me! I'm scared."

Cecilia gasped for air and mumbled, "Where's Sophia?"

Jody scrambled to the window, grabbed the plant, and handed it to her. She sat up and hugged the cracked pot holding Sophia. "I'm sorry, Jody. I'm so sorry," Cecilia cried hysterically.

"It's okay, Cece. It's all going to be okay," Jody said, trying to reassure her. "Do you want to talk about it?"

"No."

Jody went to fix some chamomile tea and came back with her Bible. "May I read to you while you're having tea?"

She sat with a blank stare for several seconds. "The Bible?"

"Yeah, if it's okay with you."

"Okay."

Jody opened her Bible to the Psalms and read Psalm 91 out loud.

"He who dwells in the secret place of the Most High shall abide under the shadow of the Almighty. I will say of the Lord, 'He is my refuge and fortress; my God, whom I trust.' Surely, He shall deliver you from the snare of the fowler and from the perilous pestilence. He shall cover you with His feathers and under His wings, you shall take refuge; His truth shall be your shield and buckler. You shall not be afraid of the terror by night, nor of the arrow that flies by day, nor of the pestilence that walks in darkness, nor of the destruction that lays waste at noonday. A thousand may fall at your side and ten thousand at your right hand, but it shall not come near you."

Before Jody could say another word, Cecilia yawned and turned over. There would be no more talk—that was enough about Jesus and God. The door shut and locked.

Jody closed her Bible, turned off the light, and crawled back into bed.

21

CECILIA WENT TO her classes the next day, fearful the police would be calling her to administration any minute or waiting outside her next class. She never heard Professor Steinbeck call her name. She sat motionless, silently interrogating herself. *How could I have been so stupid? The lady at the desk knew I was interested in RJM's painting. What if she called the police? I didn't steal it. I just threw it in the trash where it belonged. What if? What if? God, this doesn't seem too hard for you. How about it, God, or are you too busy helping someone else again?* Closing her book, she stood up and walked out of class.

Professor Steinbeck followed her out. "Cecilia, is anything wrong? You seem very distracted today. Is there anything I can do for you?"

"No, sir. I'm not feeling well, but I'll be okay," she tried to say convincingly.

"Alright. See you next week," he said, returning to the classroom.

She knew the next hurdle to overcome would be the art therapy class on Saturday. *I'm sure Judd frequents the museum with his students.* The lady at the desk would probably contact him. Cecilia tried to block it from her thoughts by staying extremely busy the next few days. She turned every conversation with Jody into a long debate, trying to escape what was really on her mind.

"Hey Cece, it's Friday night! How about we grab something from the taco food truck and see *Casablanca* at the Paramount?"

"Yes! Let's do it!"

They grabbed their jackets and headed down Congress Avenue. Jody made small talk while they sat and ate their tacos.

"Girl, is everything okay? We haven't talked much since the museum trip. You were so stressed that night."

Cecilia nodded yes and changed the subject quickly. "Thanks for getting me out of the room. Going to the movies is what I needed. You'd think we'd get tired of seeing *Casablanca*. We've only seen it like a *trillion times!*"

"Yeah, well, we better get going; we sure don't wanna miss any of it!" The line extended down the street from the theater. "Wow, everyone must have needed a Blanca fix," Jody said.

"No, probably more like cheap tickets!" Cecilia laughed.

"Hey, is that Judd up there?"

"I don't think so."

"Oh yeah, that's him alright," Jody said emphatically."

When Cecilia saw him looking in their direction, she turned away and started quoting all the movie lines to divert Jody's attention from Judd.

They both began laughing hysterically, knowing this could go on all night, for they'd memorized almost every line from the movie.

"Cecilia, straighten up now!" Jody said as they made their way to the window. "They may think we've been drinking and not let us in."

"I can't help it!"

Jody elbowed her. Cecilia grabbed her side and smiled while paying for her ticket. She was glad that Judd had already gone in. Cecilia declined Jody's offer for popcorn and hurried to find a seat away from their teacher. With no sight of him, she took a seat in the back.

When she saw Jody approaching with Judd close behind, her hands began to sweat profusely. *No way! He's not coming to sit with us!*

Jody squeezed past her, leaving room for Judd to sit between them.

"Hi, Cecilia," Judd said as he lowered himself into the chair.

Cecilia acknowledged him. Her deadpan face stared ahead as the red Paramount curtain opened to reveal the grand screen. With the lights dimmed and the movie starting, Cecilia lost herself in the moment. Her heartbeat slowed, and the smell of his cologne stirred a warm sensation she had taken captive whenever he was near. Tonight, she allowed it to go free. No thoughts of the trip to the museum were permitted. She wanted to breathe him in and pretend her past didn't exist.

The three of them blurted out all the famous lines in unison. Knowing what to expect with every scene gave her a sense of control. No surprises. She knew how this story ended. It never changed.

When the movie ended, Judd asked, "May I walk you back to the dorm since it's dark?"

"That'd be great!" Jody answered.

Cecilia nodded, feeling she had no choice since Jody had made such a big deal out of it. A flashback of RJM's painting she trashed caused her eyes to twitch.

Would he say something tonight? Did he know?

Cecilia stepped up her pace to create some space between them.

Back at the dorm, Judd said his goodbyes.

"Thanks for walking us back," Cecilia said.

"Not a problem," he said, looking deeply into her eyes.

Both girls waved goodbye and ran up the stairs. Jody quickly opened the door and began her antics.

"Cece, he likes you. Can't you see that? He can't take his eyes off you. And he's a hottie."

"Jody, stop! There are at least one hundred reasons why this isn't a good idea. For crying out loud, he's my professor! Something you keep *forgetting*. Number two, I don't wanna be in a relationship with anyone right now. Number three, you're crazy! He's not interested in me!" *And he never would be if he knew all about me.*

"All right then," she said, grinning from ear to ear. "We'll see."

Cecilia threw a pillow at Jody and turned to take a shower, leaving herself wide open for retaliation.

"Okay, girl! It's on." The pillow fight lasted until they held their arms in the air, signaling cease-fire. "You better get that hot shower and go to bed early. You know what tomorrow is," Jody teased. Cecilia grabbed another pillow and landed it on Jody's head before she darted into the bathroom and locked the door.

When she came out, Jody had her reading light on and her Bible on her chest. *You read that book every night. I'm glad it means something to you.* Bending to turn the light off, Cecilia kissed Jody on the forehead and put her Bible on the nightstand.

After getting in bed, her thoughts turned to Judd. A faint scent of his cologne lingered. *No, stop…*one hundred reasons this wouldn't work began rolling off her tongue. "I'm not ready; I'm not ready. I'm not ready one hundred times over. No. Period. Even if I were, he's not interested! I'm not the kind of girl he would want. I don't wear a *cross* around my neck."

22

"I'M GOING FOR a run. Do you wanna come with me?" Cecilia asked Jody the following day.

"No, I'm gonna get ready for class and drink my coffee!"

"I'll be back soon! Be ready!"

"I will," Jody answered with a yawn.

They made it to class just as it started. Cecilia hurried past Judd and quickly sat down.

She pulled out her pencil and began to doodle, still thinking of RJM. *Why am I letting him get under my skin?* Several people presented their papers, but Cecilia didn't hear a word. She was trapped in this bubble, which she felt would burst any second and land her in RJM's cell—alone with him, glaring into his twisted soul.

"Your next assignment is simple," he said, thrusting her back into reality. "I want you to draw any shape and then paint it with a color that makes you feel peaceful."

Peaceful? Cecilia rubbed her eyes with her clammy hands to stop the room from spinning. The thoughts of RJM had sent her into a tailspin.

Jody glanced over at Cecilia and noticed how pale she was. "Do you need some water?"

"I think I need fresh air," she said, trying to stand while her knees gave way to the floor.

She woke to Judd holding her in his arms while carrying her down the hall.

"Cecilia," Judd said with fear in his eyes. "I'm taking you to the student health center. You passed out and gave us all a scare."

Feeling secure in his arms, she closed her eyes and whispered, "I'm okay."

"It's still better to get you checked out." Judd gently lowered her and held her arm as he opened the door. Jody was right behind them.

"We'll be outside the door if you need anything," Judd said.

"Thank you," she said, thinking of him carrying her down the hall.

"Hey, do you want me to stay with you?" Jody asked.

"Let me check her out and ask a few questions, and then I'll let you come back in," the nurse interrupted.

Jody and Judd stepped back as the door slowly closed.

The nurse took Cecilia's vital signs as she asked her question after question.

"Is there a chance you might be pregnant? When was your last period?"

"No, ma'am, my period was a week ago," Cecilia said as she felt the blood draining from her face. The question triggered a sour taste in her mouth.

"Do you have diabetes?"

"No."

"When was the last time you had something to eat?" the nurse continued.

Her reaction to RJM had left her mentally exhausted and unable to eat much for several days.

"I had supper last night," *even though most of it ended up in the trash.*

The nurse checked her blood sugar and gave her orange juice and crackers. "Your blood sugar is slightly low, but your vital signs are normal. Have this snack, and let's see if you start feeling better."

"Thank you. Would you ask Jody to come back in?"

Jody quickly entered with concern on her face. "Are you okay?"

"I'm fine. Really. I just got a little hot and haven't had much appetite lately. Thanks to you, I had a fish taco and popcorn last night," she said, smiling, trying to ease the tension on Jody's face. "Hey, you're the best!

I'm glad you're my bestie," Cecilia said while thinking about how Jody always seemed to be there when she needed someone.

"Well, you should've seen Judd spring into action. He dismissed the class, scooped you into his strong arms like Mr. Prince Charming, and practically ran with you down the hall. He looked terrified. Poor guy's got it bad, Cece. Do you care if I let him come back in for a minute so he can see you're alright?"

"Oh my gosh, yes."

Judd came in and pulled up a chair right before her but remained silent.

"Thanks for helping me. I'm feeling better now," Cecilia said as she pointed to the juice and crackers. "I ran this morning and didn't get a chance to eat anything. Besides, I guess you know now I'll do anything to get out of an assignment." she said, smiling.

"Don't ever pull a stunt like that again, or you'll get a double assignment. Are you sure you're feeling okay? Do you need anything?"

Jody was behind him, shaking her head yes.

"No, I'll be fine," Cecilia said, trying not to make eye contact with Jody.

"Here," Judd said, handing her his card with his phone number. "If you do, just give me a call."

"Thank you. I'll put this on the mini fridge as a reminder to eat so I don't get any extra assignments!"

Smiling, he turned and went out the door.

"I feel better already," Cecilia said, knowing she had escaped any wrath that may have come from her meltdown with RJM's paintings.

23

TIME PASSED, AND Cecilia filed all thoughts of RJM into some deep, hidden compartment of her brain. Her mind was entirely focused on graduation. She had stayed true to herself and would graduate with a 4.0 GPA if all continued to go well. Art therapy helped her through the last semester. Being in the same room with Judd and a paintbrush in her hand felt like a vacation on a sandy beach, sitting under an umbrella with a good book and sipping lemonade. *I'm sure gonna miss this class and Judd.* He had kept things cordial, but Cecilia couldn't help but wonder if Jody was right.

Is he really into me?

Judd announced the upcoming art contest and silent auction on Saturday before graduation. "I encourage all of you to enter. The first prize is ten thousand dollars, the second is five thousand dollars, and the third is two thousand five hundred dollars. The winning artist will bring home the prize money and all money made from the sale. Is anyone interested?" Cecilia and Jody raised their hands enthusiastically. Judd smiled as he handed them papers with details of the event and submission instructions. Back at the dorm, Cecilia pulled the flyer out of her backpack and read aloud, "Ten thousand dollars for first place, five thousand dollars for second place, and two thousand five hundred dollars for third place. Wow. Okay. I probably don't stand a chance, but I'm gonna give it a shot. I could use some extra cash."

"Me too!"

"Speaking of extra cash, I have to go," Cecilia groaned. "I'm tutoring this annoying freshman at one o'clock!"

"Hey, but listen before you go. I've got a great idea. I've seen some people sitting in the Zilker Botanical Gardens with their easels, painting—you know, like real artists. You wanna see if we can pull it off? You know, *look* like *real artists*."

"Sure! I'm free this Friday afternoon."

"We only have a few more classes with you know who," Jody teased.

"Don't you go there!"

"How can you be so cold, or should I say, indifferent to him? You know he's crazy about you."

"Jody, stop it. I start law school soon. I don't need any distractions. I have to focus. I've come too far to get sidetracked with a relationship now. Besides, a guy that wears a cross around his neck surely wouldn't want anything to do with me."

"Wait a minute now. Ma'am, you need to take the stand. Tell me, how could someone with a cross on her dresser and a Bible on her nightstand ever become your best friend?"

"Objection, your honor. It's not the same."

"How so?"

Cecilia shook her head. "It's just not the same. You love me unconditionally. You don't expect me to be anyone other than who I am. You don't *expect* anything from me. You see the best in me. You let me be me."

Jody looked at her and slowly began to speak. "You know, girlfriend, Jesus loves you much more than I could ever love you, and that's an awful lot. He loved you so much, He died on a cross for you."

Cecilia's jaw tensed, "I never asked him to do that."

Jody's face twinged.

Cecilia quickly said, "Hey, I'm sorry. Don't tell me how much Jesus loves me or anything else about him. Judd can't love me, really love me, because I don't love his God."

"I understand, Cecilia. Enough said. Just know I love you like a sister, and you're the best friend I've ever had."

"I'm gonna miss you. I don't know what I would've done or how

I would've made it through school without you. You've always been there for me. I know I haven't been the kind of friend you deserve. Anyway, I just wanna say thank you."

"You're acting as if we'll never see each other again. Who knows? We may be partners in bringing justice to all our high-paying clients!"

"High-paying clients? I would like that, and it would be even better if we were law partners."

Deep down, Cecilia prepared herself to be on the journey alone, once again. The closer she got to graduation, the more her past haunted her. Her university life was a facade. It was a fake life because no one knew who she was and the darkness hiding inside her. Jody was the only one she had ever let see even a glimpse of her soiled past.

O N FRIDAY, JODY met Cecilia and her faithful potted plant, Soph, at the front gate of the botanical gardens.

"Did you check her in? They may think you stole her, and you don't have enough money for me to take the case. Besides, 'jailbird' or 'thief' wouldn't look good on your resume!"

"Ha ha," Cecilia smirked. Sophia had grown so much she'd been transplanted into a larger pot, almost too big to be carried.

"Here, put this sleep mask on, and trust me. I have a surprise for you."

"You're asking a lot, girlfriend. Trusting you to lead me around blindfolded while carrying my most prized possession!"

"Don't be a wimp. Just do it. I'll take her. You hold my hand, and we'll go slowly. It's not too far."

"What's not too far?"

"You'll see!"

Cecilia did as she was told, carefully taking baby steps.

Jody stopped and put the plant down. "Are you ready?"

"Yes!!! Past ready!"

"Okay, then. Let me help you with the mask, but keep your eyes closed until I say open!"

Cecilia squinted her eyes and kept them closed while Jody removed the mask.

"On the count of three, open your eyes. One, two, and three!"

Cecilia opened her eyes to see two beautiful wooden easels, two chairs, paintbrushes, paints, and two aprons that said "ART THERAPY...paint your story."

"I wanted to get something special for my best friend for graduation. Cecilia, don't ever think you haven't been a good friend; you're my *best* friend. I know you don't like to talk about God, but your friendship has been and is my gift from God."

Tears flowed as they hugged.

"Jody, this is the loveliest gift anyone has ever given me. Wow! Thank you so much!"

Jody pulled a tissue out of her pocket, blew her nose, and said, "Okay, let's get to work now and create those prize-winning masterpieces."

"The best prize is sitting here painting with you."

"Does that mean you'll give me the prize money if you win?" Jody asked while grinning big.

"I wouldn't go that far!"

Neither girl spoke a word for the next few hours. They kept painting until Cecilia felt a few raindrops on her arms.

"Quickly, Jody, put the paints in my bag, and let's get everything to the car. We'll have to run!" The downpour started just as they reached the parking lot. Sitting in the car, they watched as bolts of lightning sparked across the sky.

"Whoa! I think it's time to go!" Jody said.

Cecilia helped unload and put everything back in the dorm room. "I'm so glad our paintings didn't get wet. That would've been tragic! I'm gonna change and get out of these wet clothes. If you like, we can go grab something to eat."

"Yes! I'm starving."

Cecilia came out of the bathroom with her hair still wrapped in a towel. "Hey, where's Sophie? Jody, did we leave her at the park? Oh, my god!" she cried hysterically.

Jody froze. "I don't see her. Come on, I'll drive you back. I'm sure she's okay," she said, trying to reassure Cecilia as she watched her face grow pale.

"No, no, no, this isn't happening!" Cecilia cried as an overwhelming sensation of dread grabbed her by the throat.

"Come on, let's get in the car and find her. We're wasting time here, Cece."

Cecilia flinched when Jody took hold of her arm. "Everything will be okay," Cecilia repeated over and over again as she struggled to contain her hysteria.

Jody pulled up to the front entrance to let her out. "I'll park the car. At least the rain has finally stopped. You go on now."

Cecilia ran back to where they had been and anxiously scanned the area. "Sophia, I'm sorry I left you. Where are you?" she cried, falling to the ground. "You are mine. You're for my garden!"

"Lady, do you need some help?" asked the groundskeeper, who had come in his golf cart to check on her.

Cecilia's body began to tremble as she wrapped her arms around herself and rocked back and forth, sobbing.

"Here, let me help you up." He extended his hand to her.

"I have to find my plant," she cried. "I left it here when the rain started, and it's gone now."

"I might have what you're looking for."

"Do you have Sophia?"

"I'm not sure if I have Sophia, but one of the gardeners found a plant on the grounds earlier and told me he'd put it in the greenhouse. He said it turned over during the storm, and the pot got cracked. I thought I knew all the gardeners, but I'd never seen him before. He said he was covering for someone. Hop in, and I'll take you there."

Without hesitation, Cecilia climbed into the golf cart and rode with him a short distance to the greenhouse. He walked over to a table where a broken pot lay with its dirt and plant strewn about. "The gardener said someone would come looking for this."

"Oh, my god," she said as she tried scooping Sophia and the dirt back into the broken pot.

"Wait, I have a pot in here you can have," he said, trying to calm her. "Let me help you get it planted again. Your plant is safe, miss! Let's put a little fresh dirt in here. A special plant like this shouldn't live in a broken pot," he said, smiling.

Cecilia began to cry. "Oh, my god. I thought I'd lost her forever. This plant *is* special. It's been with me for a long time. I don't know what I would've done if something had happened to her."

"What kind of plant is this? I've never seen anything like it before."

"It's my angel plant."

"Well, how about that? An angel plant! It's all planted again and looks happy in its new home." The sun shone through the greenhouse door. "Do you and your plant need a ride on the golf cart somewhere?"

"Oh, my gosh! Jody must be beside herself. Yes, please, would you take me back to my friend? She's at the park entrance. We were painting when it started to rain. We were running with everything, and I forgot my plant." Cecilia climbed into the golf cart. "I'm sorry I was rude to you. It's just that this plant is important to me, and for a moment, I thought it was gone."

"It's not a problem. I know how people can get attached to their plants!" he said, smiling at her again.

Jody stood by the entrance and ran to meet them when she saw Cecilia in the golf cart.

"I see you found it. Thanks a lot," Jody said as the man helped Cecilia out with her plant.

"Thanks again, sir," Cecilia said. "I appreciate all your help."

Cecilia got in the car with Sophie on her lap. "Whew, that was a close one!"

"Cece?"

"Yeah."

"I'm worried about you. I know this plant is important to you, but the hysteria I saw in you when Sophia was missing was over the top. I've noticed that every time something upsets you, the only thing that seems to calm you down is your plant."

Cecilia offered a fake smile. "Hey, we should probably get back to the dorm and drop Sophia off so we can get something to eat," she said, trying to change the subject.

When Cecilia's eyes darted out the window, Jody could see her body bristle.

"Cece, I'm concerned about you. That's all. When I told you about my rape and the abortion, you got up and grabbed Sophia so you could hold her. When you woke up during the night from a nightmare, you wanted to hold Sophia. Please tell me what's going on. Maybe I can help you. Trust me."

"You think I'm crazy, don't you?"

"No."

"Okay, I'll tell you, and then you'll think I am."

Jody shook her head no as she reached over to put her hand on Cecilia's shoulder. "It might help if you talk about it." Cecilia briefly closed her eyes as she quietly exhaled, recalling the memory she had protected for so long. "When I was sixteen, I was digging in my backyard, in the scorching sun, to plant a garden. I was devastated about the possibility of being pregnant and pounded the earth so hard that I must've passed out in the heat. The next morning, I woke up in the hospital. The nurse told me *my guardian* had called an ambulance and rode in with me."

"Guardian?" Jody interjected.

Without missing a beat, Cecilia continued, "She said he sat by my bed the whole night and left in the early morning. He came back before shift change and left the plant. It was one of the first things I saw when I woke up. That was the day I learned I was pregnant. This *guardian* left enough money in my account to pay for the entire hospital bill. He told the nurse he didn't want me to worry about anything. He said the plant was for my garden." She paused. "So, I named it Sophia."

"Did you ever find out who this guardian was?"

"No, but a strange man would sometimes show up, and I wondered if it was him. The night I got pregnant and was left alone on the beach, a man reached for my hand when I tried making my way up the stairs in the dark. Then, he just disappeared. All along my way to Texas, a man would show up here and there that I felt I had seen before, and then he would be gone."

"He sounds like an angel."

"I'm not sure what I think about angels. I don't know how to explain it. But one thing is certain: Sophie's been the only tangible thing I could hold onto and even talk to when I couldn't talk to anyone else," Cecilia said with a nervous laugh. "I know this sounds crazy and bizarre, but now you have it."

"Cece, that's beautiful, and I don't think you're crazy. We all have ways we process things in life. It's okay. I'm here and want you to know that you can talk to me about anything, anytime you need to." Jody reached over to hug her. Pulling away, smiling, she added, "A guardian, huh? That's pretty awesome!"

"Yeah, right," Cecilia replied, managing to smile back.

25

I N THE MORNING, Cecilia awoke with a nagging desire to revisit the museum.

Trying to shake it, she pulled the covers over her head, closed her eyes tightly, and started to hum an old song. Nothing worked.

She dressed, grabbed her purse, and left for the art museum before she lost her nerve. She hadn't been there since the field trip. Her legs grew weak as she thought of the myriad of emotions she had for RJM after discovering he was on death row for murder. *Why am I going there?*

Her breathing became faster with every deliberate footstep she took. She made her way up the steps, opened the door, signed in, and walked right past the lady behind the desk and straight to where RJM's artwork had hung. She exhaled loudly, realizing she had been holding her breath since pushing through the front entrance. She had to see for herself. *Was it still there? Did someone find it in the trash? Oh, my god! It's here. How did it get back on the wall?* She sat on the slick white bench before the painting, trying to understand why it made her so angry.

"Cecilia, I didn't expect to see you here."

Surprised by Judd's appearance, Cecilia said hello and returned to the painting, trying not to appear rattled.

"Mind if I sit here beside you?"

"Sure." She could feel the warmth radiating from his body. The smell of his cologne was intoxicating.

"What do you see, Cecilia?" Judd asked, breaking the silence.

She stood up with her eyes glued to the painting. "I'm not sure, but it makes me angry."

Not wanting to discuss the artwork anymore, Cecilia turned to leave. It had been put back in its place, and that was all she needed to know.

"Hey," he said. "I'm going for a walk in Zilker Park. Would you like to come? It's lunchtime."

"Zilker Park?"

He had caught her attention. Cecilia loved going to that park. It had become her happy place since coming to the University of Texas. Many called it the jewel in the heart of Austin. She loved the kite festival in the spring, the Christmas tree lighting in December, canoeing with Jody, and especially the blues music they often played on the greens— so many good memories.

"Yes," she answered. "I'd like that. Jody and I went to the Botanical Gardens last Friday to paint."

"I'm impressed. Artists on the move. I bet that was nice."

"It was until the rain came!"

"Well, the sun is shining today. My car's outside," he said. "Are you okay riding with me?"

"Why wouldn't I be?"

"You know, with me being your teacher."

"It's just a walk in the park. It's *not* a date! You're just helping me with my art assignment," she laughed.

"Right!"

The talk was light, and Judd's dry sense of humor kept her laughing all the way to the park. She felt free to be herself briefly without fear of something terrible happening. The day was beautiful and sunny. Judd went around the car to open her door and extended his hand to help her out.

"Well, thank you kindly, sir!" she said in her most southern accent.

"You're quite welcome," he said while taking a bow.

Cecilia giggled like some young schoolgirl as they walked through the park.

"Would ya like a hot dog?" Judd asked.

"Sure. Mustard and ketchup, please."

"I like a girl who knows what she wants!"

Handing her the hot dog, they found a park bench and sat down.

"The sun feels marvelous!" she said while closing her eyes and laying her head back to catch the warmth of its rays on her face.

Her soul felt his penetrating gaze. Trying to contain her runaway imaginings, she quickly sat up and removed the foil from her hotdog.

"Thanks. What do I owe you?"

"Nothing, my treat."

"Thank you," she said, looking down at her toes. *What will he do when he knows the truth? I need to tell him.*

They found a grassy spot to sit, and Judd remained quiet, allowing Cecilia to express her thoughts.

"Judd, I should have come to you sooner, but I was afraid."

"Afraid? Well, I'm here now."

"I need to tell you about something I did when we visited the museum as a class. That day, I was intrigued by RJM's artwork. When I inquired about the artist, I learned he was in prison, on death row for murder, and his artwork was donated or sold for charity. I had left the museum with Jody, but something snapped as I thought about him displaying his art."

Cecilia looked away.

Judd gently guided her chin back to him. "It's okay. You can talk to me."

"I'm humiliated. I went back into the museum, consumed with anger. I took RJM's painting from the wall and threw it in the bathroom trash. I figured someone would come looking for me since I had inquired about the artist. I thought the lady at the desk would find me since we were there as your students. I was afraid I'd be arrested, and it would ruin my chances of getting into law school. I haven't been able to concentrate since."

Judd didn't speak but continued to listen intently.

"The only relief I had was when we were all at the movies that night. I wasn't sure if you knew and was so thankful you didn't mention anything when you walked us back to the dorm."

"Is that why you kept trying to get away from me?"

"Yeah, I guess so. I dreaded your class the next day, thinking you were waiting to confront me. I guess the stress of it all and not being able to eat caused me to pass out. I'm so sorry and ashamed."

Judd reached for her hand, and she willingly accepted. "I didn't know if you would come to me, so I planned on talking to you after class last week. Instead, I carried you to the Student Health Center and didn't think it was the appropriate time."

"You knew?"

"I was there that night in the exhibit beside you. I thought all the students had left. I knew that painting triggered some deep emotions within you. I heard you crying through the bathroom door, so I waited for you to come out but never saw you."

"I felt like a thief trying to escape and left as quietly as possible."

"I saw the painting was missing and opened the bathroom door, only to see it hanging out of the trashcan. I returned it where it belonged. No one saw me," Judd said.

"Oh, my god! If they had, they could have accused you of taking it."

"It's okay. No one did. I was relieved to see you at the movie theater. I've been worried about you."

Cecilia looked at him in unbelief. "Why did you do that for me? Why did you cover for me?" Cecilia was used to people, especially men, taking from her.

"I heard the distress and anguish in your voice. I care for you, Cecilia."

"I'm shocked. I haven't told anyone, not even Jody. I didn't want to bring her into this." "Do you wanna tell me what made you want to destroy the art?"

"I can't. It's too much." She put her face in her hands and began to cry.

"Hey, it's alright," he said, wrapping his arm around her shoulder and handing her a napkin to wipe her eyes. "If you need to talk, I'm a good listener."

It was blues day in the park, and the band began to play the song, "You Are So Beautiful."

Judd took her hand and pulled her in closely. Her heart was

pounding as he whispered in her ear, "May I have this dance?" She loved everything about him: his touch, his smell, his dark eyes, the kind way he talked to her. Without resistance, she melted in his arms as he began to sing along with the song.

"Cecilia, you *are* beautiful. I hope you understand that. Everything about you is beautiful."

She felt herself pulling away from him. The voices in her head taunted her. *Who do you think you are, Cecilia? He could never love you. You are a nobody. Go ahead, Cecilia, tell him!*

He reached down to kiss her, and with a knee-jerk reaction, she slapped his face. Cecilia froze briefly when she saw her hand imprinted on his cheek and then took off running as fast as she could.

Judd called after her, "Cecilia, I'm sorry. Please come back."

"I'm not good for you!" She began to run faster until she reached the steps of her dorm.

She knew Jody would ask too many questions that she didn't want to answer, so she found a shady bench under the oak tree and lay down to think instead of going in.

What have I done? What's wrong with me? The sun had set when Cecilia finally decided to go inside. *I guess he'll leave me alone now.* Her heart sank as she played the scene of him holding her close and softly singing.

Me, beautiful? If you only knew, Judd.

THE NEXT DAY, Cecilia heard some noise at the door and opened it only to find a note taped there with her name on it. Stuffing it into her pocket, she grabbed her things to leave.

"See ya later, Jody," she yelled through the bathroom door, and hurried off to a more private place between the buildings to read the note.

Dear Cecilia,

Please forgive me. I was out of line. I realize I'm your professor, and I know I was out of order doing what I did, but I felt like it was a moment we both wanted. The afternoon was emotionally charged. It was a lot to process mentally and emotionally. I was insensitive to your needs. The timing was wrong, but my desire to kiss and hold you was real. Please don't shut the door to the possibility of something good happening with us. Let me in. You can trust me. Don't worry about the museum. The painting wasn't harmed. Cecilia, I hope you will one day feel safe with me. Please give me a chance to prove that to you.

Judd

Insensitive to my needs? she thought. *Who talks like that? No one's ever cared about my needs. Why are you so nice to me? Yes, Judd. I did want you to kiss me, but if you knew who I was, you wouldn't want to kiss me. I don't deserve you. Most of all, I need to prove that I can get through college and law school on my own. You can't get in the way of that. Don't you understand? Maybe when I'm successful, all the other junk from my past won't matter so much. Perhaps then, I'll be good enough for you to love.*

26

SATURDAY CAME. JODY sat at the table, eating a bowl of Lucky Charms and chattering about the art contest.

Cecilia only had one thing on her mind at that moment. *How am I ever going to face Judd?* Throwing her backpack on, she headed for the door.

"Hey, aren't ya gonna wait for me?" Jody asked.

"Oh, sorry, my mind's thinking about everything I need to get done before graduation."

"Like finishing that picture to put in the contest," Jody said, smiling.

"For sure! It would be nice to have all that money to tide us over until we make the big bucks!"

Still, the knot in her stomach was getting tighter and tighter as she felt the phantom sting of her palm slapping Judd's face. The sting must have paled compared to the hurt she had seen in his eyes.

"I'm ready; let's get this done!" Jody said triumphantly.

Cecilia was glad that Judd was talking to a student when she got to class. She took her seat and pulled out a notebook and pen, hoping to look busy or, even better, invisible.

After the last student arrived, Judd took attendance and stood up behind his desk. "How many of you are entering the art contest?" he asked. Every hand went up. "This is the most prize money that's ever been given by a private donor from the museum, and I'm pleased to see all of you entering. Do you also plan on allowing your piece to be auctioned off?" Again, every hand went up.

"Wonderful. Since there's only two classes left, I thought we'd go outside and paint. You may use class time to work on your contest piece or something else. Everyone grab an easel and chair and meet me in the side yard."

Cecilia gathered everything she needed and headed to the door.

I sure hope this isn't gonna be weird.

While everyone was painting, Judd talked to the students, giving compliments and suggestions. He stopped for a moment by Cecilia's easel. "Nice work."

Cecilia froze. She wanted to look at him but kept her eyes glued to the painting. There was an awkward silence. Deep down, she longed for him to touch her shoulder and whisper in her ear, "You're so beautiful to me." Then it was over. He had moved on.

Two weeks from now, I won't be your student. Judd, could you love me if you knew the truth about my awful past?

Cecilia shifted her thoughts back to the painting and suddenly felt a kaleidoscope of emotions sweep over her. *I'm sorry I hurt you. I was so mean, and then you asked me to forgive you. You never even judged me for throwing the painting in the trash. You covered the wrong thing I did so no one would know. Judd Taylor, I've never known a man like you.*

Cecilia dipped her brush into the crimson red paint, and with the ease of each stroke she applied to the canvas, her painting began to sing. The colors morphed into freedom. There was no anxiety. No fear. Everything bad washed away as she twirled her brush in the water before adding a new, vibrant color.

"I'm leaving, Cece," Jody said.

Engrossed in her painting, Cecilia waved goodbye with her free hand without looking up. Her desire to dress the canvas couldn't be thwarted until Judd touched her shoulder. Looking up, she melted into his dark brown eyes.

"Everyone's gone."

"Could we stay a little longer?" she pleaded. "I need to finish this."

"Alright. Take your time. I have some things I can do." He sat under the oak tree and began to work on something.

Cecilia felt safe being far enough away from him to resist the urge to do anything that proximity might evoke.

She put her brush into the water container and dipped her fingers in the paint, applying it to the canvas in a way that made her painting sing of new life.

Looking up, she caught Judd staring in her direction. He walked over and sat down on the ground.

"If only this painting could talk."

"I hope it speaks to you. Judd, listen, I'm sor—"

"It does," he interrupted before she could finish her apology. He reached for her hand and said, "It gives me hope for us."

"Stop!" she yelled, lifting her hand from his grip. "I just tried to apologize for slapping you. What are you doing? I have to go."

I can't do this. I'm not who you think I am. If only you knew.

She grabbed the painting and her bag.

"Cecilia, don't leave like this. I'm sorry."

"Goodbye, Judd. I can't do this! And stop saying you're sorry!"

CECILIA DEBATED ALL week whether to attend her last art therapy class or skip it. Saturday morning came, and she decided to go since Judd hadn't tried to contact her in any way.

She followed closely behind Jody as they entered the classroom and took their seats, never looking toward him. Things appeared back to normal, at least on the surface. She was relieved that he wasn't confronting her or making her uncomfortable. She watched as he straightened a stack of papers on his desk at least ten times.

"Did everyone turn in their pieces to the art council on time?" Judd asked as he scanned the room for a show of hands. "Good," he said as he began straightening the papers again.

I'm glad he seems uncomfortable.

Cecilia turned to Jody to keep from staring at Judd. "I'll be glad when Saturday gets here. It feels so strange not having my painting around. Seriously, I feel connected to it. That angel plant has seen me through some *tough* times."

My guardian wanted me to have a garden. He knew I needed Sophia. Cecilia remembered the first time she saw the plant on the windowsill at the hospital when she was pregnant and afraid. The plant had survived the trip to Austin and the night she'd almost died on those train tracks.

"Well, if you win, it will see you through some *good* times!" Jody said.

"There you go with the *ifs* again." Cecilia laughed out loud, thinking about how Jody had prayed over their art before handing it to the council.

"What's so funny?" Jody asked.

"Well, didn't you pray that God would let this art speak to someone's heart and bring healing and restoration to their broken soul? And it would be okay with us if it's one or both of ours."

"I'm impressed, Cece. You remembered my prayer."

"Ha ha. No, seriously now, letting go of that painting was like letting go of a part of Sophia somehow. I can't explain it. I just know that painting Soph in that picturesque garden gave me hope that all the horror in my life might turn into some beautiful song. Maybe it will bring that same hope to someone whose life is painting a picture of gloom and doom."

"Is that why you named it *When Darkness Sings—Redemption's Melody?*"

"I suppose so."

27

"**C**OME ON! GET up!" Cecilia opened the shades and made a noise so Jody would wake up.

"Girl, what in the world?"

"Today's the day for Sophia to shine! Now, hurry up!"

"Okay, alright! Just let me brush my teeth, will ya?"

"Aren't you excited, Jody? I can't believe the art show is finally here."

"I am, Cece, but I don't think there's anyone as excited about this as you are!"

Cecilia smiled. "Painting makes me happy. There's something about dipping your fingers in paint and gliding it across the canvas. If you mess up, you can just paint right over it until something beautiful emerges, like the caterpillar's metamorphosis into an exquisite butterfly. And today, Sophia gets to fly! I love it."

"Wow, Cece! That's deep. And just think how you would never have experienced such happiness if your good pal here hadn't talked you into art therapy class!"

"Ha ha! You're right, though. And for that, I will forever be indebted to you!"

"You can start with dinner and a movie if you win all that prize money."

"*If* I win??? Maybe you should pray again!"

"Okay, *when* you win!" Jody laughed.

"Now, let's go!"

THE GIRLS RODE their bikes to Zilker Park and locked them in the bike rack.

"Hurry, Jody, let's go find our place!"

"Can a girl catch her breath, please? You're killing me!" Jody said as Cecilia eagerly ran ahead. Hundreds of canvases lined the walkway. Jody spotted her painting first and noticed Cecilia standing several feet away, staring at hers. A heavy cloud descended around Cecilia. The despair on her face propelled Jody to her side.

"Cece, what's wrong?"

She pointed to the painting beside hers. "Is this a joke? Who would do this to me?"

Beside Cecilia's *When Darkness Sings* was the cryptic abstract signed by RJM. Jody had no chance to say anything before Cecilia took off running.

She tried to catch her, but Cecilia was not one to be *caught* when she didn't want to be.

"I need to be alone!"

Jody stopped dead in her tracks.

Cecilia unlocked her bike and made her way through the maze of people. She slammed on brakes to keep from hitting Judd as he crossed the street.

"Did *you* do it?" she demanded.

"Do what, Cecilia?"

"Display my art next to RJM's?"

"No. Cecilia, I don't know what you're talking about. I promise."

"I don't believe you!" she shouted while riding away.

JODY KNOCKED ON the dorm door to warn Cecilia before she turned the key to let herself in at the end of the day. "Is it okay to come in?"

"Sure, Jody.

Cecilia was sitting by the window, staring out.

I'm sorry. It happened again. I'm always running from something."

Jody set her book bag down and sat on the couch close to her. "Cece, what are you running from?"

"It doesn't matter."

"Please don't push me away. I love you."

Cecilia's gaze moved from the window to Jody's eyes. "I think that's what I'm running from."

"Love?"

"It's hard to explain. I just don't believe I can be loved."

"But I'm telling you that I love you. You don't believe that?"

She paused and then said, "I don't trust love."

"I'm sorry, Cece."

"RJM's artwork provokes something in me that makes me feel out of control. I can't handle it. It ruined everything. I felt like my picture was being violated just being beside his. I wanted to take it and run but couldn't even do that. I had to get out of there. Then, I almost ran over Judd and accused him of putting the paintings next to each other." Cecilia choked back tears. "When, Jody? When will I be free from this torment? I'm so tired of running."

Jody sat beside her friend and wrapped her arms around her. "I'm here, Cece, and even when I'm not, I'll just be a phone call away. I love you, girl. Trust me. You will get through this. Please talk to someone. There are people trained to help you."

Cecilia shook her head yes but knew she never would. She was an overcomer, and she would overcome this too…alone.

28

"It's happening, Cece," Jody said. "Tomorrow we will walk across that stage! Get your bag, and let's meet my mom and dad at the hotel."

"I still can't believe they got us a room at that fancy hotel they're staying in."

"Believe it! And believe me, we're gonna have some fun!" Jody said, with a big grin on her face.

Mrs. Hines was adamant about including Cecilia in all their family's graduation celebrations, knowing her parents weren't coming. Cecilia's dad wasn't one for traveling after getting out of the army and had sworn he'd never get on an airplane again. Of course, Mama wouldn't leave him at home.

It's been four years since I pulled out of their driveway without so much as one goodbye from him. It's okay; nobody's coming.

Cecilia's mind drifted toward Judd. *Not one word from him. He must think I'm crazy.*

Jody's parents met them at the hotel desk. After exchanging hellos and hugs, Mrs. Hines smiled and asked, "Are you girls ready to have some fun after all your hard work?"

Both girls laughed. "What's fun?"

"Shopping!"

The Hines were wealthy landowners, and money didn't seem to

be of any concern. Jody never talked much about money but never spent any frivolously. She always gave it to someone in need instead of spending it on herself. Cecilia practically had to fight to pick up the check whenever they went out to eat.

"Come on now, let's get you checked in, and then meet me in room 510. We're going to have a girl's day out. My gift to the two of you! How do manicures, pedicures, facials, massages, and some new clothes sound?" asked Mrs. Hines.

Cecilia's jaw tightened. She didn't want to owe anyone anything. *Why would she want to do all this for me? What does she want from me?*

Mrs. Hines noticed Cecilia's hesitation. "I won't take no for an answer, either!"

This paranoia has to stop. I hate thinking the worst about everyone. Mrs. Hines, of all people? What's wrong with me?

"Jody can never take no for an answer, either. Mrs. Hines, you would be an excellent attorney, just like your daughter's gonna be!"

Mr. Hines said, "Under no circumstances have I been able to win a case with her."

Mrs. Hines stood behind him and planted a big kiss on his forehead, leaving traces of her red lipstick. "You're just a big pushover," she laughed. "Now, girls, go check out your room and make sure it's to your satisfaction."

"Thanks, Mom! We'll get you in a few minutes after we drop off our bags."

Jody slid the card into the card reader and opened the door.

"Wow! This is nice! Oh, my gosh! Cece, look at the beautiful roses!" Two vases of long-stemmed wired yellow roses sat on the round table by the window. "The yellow rose of Texas just for us, Cece!" Jody pulled out the card with her name on it and read aloud, "Jeremiah 29:11: 'For I know the plans I have for you,' declares the Lord, 'plans to prosper you and not to harm you, plans to give you hope and a future.' Mom used to tell me that all the time. Read yours!"

Cecilia took her card out and read, "Psalm 139: 13-16: 'For you created my inmost being; you knit me together in my mother's womb. I praise you because I am fearfully and wonderfully made; your works are wonderful, I know that full well. My frame was not hidden from you when I was made in the secret place when I was woven together in the depths of the earth. Your eyes saw my unformed body; all the days for me were written in your book before one of them came to be.' God has a plan for your life, Cecilia, and it's good. You were born for such a time as this. I believe you will help many people! Love, Mrs. Hines." Cecilia laid the card on the table and turned away so Jody wouldn't notice the tears in her eyes. "That's nice of your mom, Jody."

"She likes you, Cece."

"Yeah, I like her, too. You're fortunate to have such fine parents." *Why couldn't I have been born into a family like hers? I guess you wanted me to suffer for some reason. Well, I'd like to know what that reason was, God.*

Jody gave her a quick hug.

"Hey, let's go get her before she starts calling."

Mrs. Hines greeted the girls at the door with more hugs.

"Mom and Dad, thank you so much for the gorgeous roses and the room!"

Cecilia added, "Yes, thank you both. The roses are stunning."

"We're so proud of you," Mrs. Hines said as she grabbed her purse. "Now, let's go hit the town."

Mr. Hines had propped himself up on the bed. He pulled his ball cap over his eyes, yawned, and said, "You girls have a great time. I'm gonna close my eyes and get a little cat nap."

Cecilia could tell he was thrilled they were all leaving so he could get some rest.

"Call me if you run out of money," he laughed.

"Girls, this is your day! Anything you want is yours. You've worked so hard, and I *want* to spoil you."

"I'd rather not get a massage, but it's fine if you two want one," Cecilia said. *Yuck, it makes me cringe to think of someone I don't know putting their hands on me.*

"That would probably take too much of our shopping time," Mrs. Hines winked.

Cecilia looked down.

Mrs. Hines raised Cecilia's chin with her two fingers and looked into her eyes.

"This is my pleasure, Cecilia. I *want* to do this. Now, don't you rob me of my pleasure!"

Jody grinned at Cecilia. "Girlfriend, you *don't* know who you're dealing with!"

Cecilia laughed and felt more at ease trying on all the clothes. She couldn't remember having anyone dote on her like Mrs. Hines did.

"That's cute, girl! Get it! You look like a million bucks. Every successful female lawyer needs at least one little black dress. Now, let's find those to-die-for red stilettos and some jewelry. You might just wear this on your first real date with Judd."

"Jody, let's not go there."

"Hmmm, we'll see!"

They ended their shopping extravaganza at Bristle's Coffee Shop, sipping caramel macchiatos before returning to the hotel.

"Did you girls have fun today?" Mrs. Hines asked.

"Mom, you outdid yourself. It's a good thing we saved those pedicures and manicures for last. At least we were able to sit for a while and recover!"

Cecilia laughed. "That's probably more shopping than we've done in the last four years! Thank you so much."

"You girls are welcome! I couldn't think of a better way to spend the day before you two beauties walk across that stage."

Mrs. Hines helped the girls carry packages up to their room.

"I better get up there and check on your dad. He might be a little hangry. If you want anything, order room service!"

Jody and Cecilia told Mrs. Hines goodnight as she grabbed them for another hug.

They talk like they're best friends and hug all the time. Mama, I don't remember you ever hugging me. Did you?

"Thank you for this most wonderful day," Mrs. Hines said. "We'll meet you downstairs for breakfast at eight. Tomorrow's the big day!"

"Thanks, Mom."

"Thank you, Mrs. Hines. I can't begin to tell you how much this day has meant to me," Cecilia said with tears in her eyes.

"Okay, enough mush. We have to get some beauty sleep," Jody interjected. Laughter echoed in the hall as they closed their door.

That night, Cecilia and Jody stayed up late, reminiscing about their last four years at UT. They went to sleep chanting the University of Texas school motto.

What starts here changes the world!

29

CECILIA WOKE EARLY and slipped downstairs while leaving Jody asleep. She called Mama's cell phone, hoping she would answer. "Hello."

Thank God it's you, Mama. I sure couldn't take Daddy jabbing a dagger in my heart again right before I walked across the stage.

"Hi, it's Cecilia."

Silence.

"Are you there?"

"Yes, I woke up thinking about you today. You did it, Cecilia. I knew you would," she said in a crackling, timbered voice.

"Mama, I wanted to call and thank you for the money you gave me when I left home and what you sent me during the years here. It wasn't easy, but it helped more than you'll ever know. I do wish you could be here, but I understand."

Mama was quiet.

Please don't start crying, Mama! "Everything's good here, Mama. I've been hanging out with Jody and her parents. Her mom took us shopping all day yesterday. It was fun. They're waiting for me to eat breakfast with them, so I need to go. Tell Daddy, tell him *nothing,*" she said, choking back tears. "Maybe I can come see you before too long. I have to go, Mama. I love you."

"I love you too, Cecilia. I'm proud of you."

CECILIA MET JODY and her family in the fancy hotel dining room. After breakfast, they returned to the dorm, unloaded all the new loot from the day before, and put on their caps and gowns.

In the bathroom mirror, Cecilia studied the reflection of her sad eyes staring back.

It's pathetic I have no family here. I sent the graduation invitations thinking at least you and Ana might come, Josh. Fifteen hundred miles wasn't far enough to escape all the hurt and abuse. All the lies. The cover-ups. There was so much pain. Mama, I had to get away to survive! I only spoke to him once in four years and felt awful for weeks. I can't imagine how you feel, Mama. I'm sorry you felt like you had to stay. I wish you were here, Daddy, so you could see that you couldn't stop me from doing something with my life, no matter how hard you tried!

She opened her purse, put some pink lipstick on, and smacked her lips defiantly.

Cecilia closed her eyes. *Why are thoughts of him hounding me now? Is it because of Jody's parents being here? I worked so hard to gain approval from you!!! Why? Well, I don't need approval from you anymore!*

"Hey, you in there? We better get a move on, or we'll be late!" Jody called.

"Ready," Cecilia said, opening the bathroom door. "We did this! We did it together! I just wish we were going to law school together. What am I gonna do here without you?"

"You could always go to the great University of North Carolina Law School with me!" Jody said.

"And give up Texas barbecue?!" Cecilia said, trying to keep it together. The thought of Jody leaving was almost more than she could bear, but she couldn't consider moving back to North Carolina. It would be much too close to Daddy.

"Now I know where your loyalty lies!"

CECILIA AND JODY went to the Frank Irwin Center and found their place in the lineup.

The pomp and circumstance began, and then the march. Judd passed by in his regalia, looking sexier than ever. *Why did he have to look so good?*

The ceremony continued with the presentation of the colors and the singing of the "Star Spangled Banner."

With everyone seated, Cecilia shifted in her chair as she nervously waited to be called to speak. Her sweaty palms dampened her rolled-up speech. She could hear Mama's voice telling her how proud she was.

Mama, I miss you. I feel so alone. Josh, why didn't you bring her? Why didn't you come? And Ana? I knew Daddy wouldn't come, and I could care less, but what about y'all? A single tear rolled down her cheek. She sat trance-like until Judd walked on the stage and began to speak.

"Ladies and gentlemen, we don't usually do this, but we have an unusual situation with one of our students this year. Our art therapy class participates in the city's annual art contest. For the first time ever, a student from our school has won first prize. Not only did the painting win the first prize of ten thousand dollars, but it was also sold to the highest bidder at fifteen thousand dollars. In addition, this student is graduating *summa cum laude* with highest honors today and a GPA of 4.0. She will also be attending law school here in the fall." Judd picked up the first-place ribbon and calmly spoke into the microphone. "Cecilia Evans, would you please come and receive your award?" The crowd stood, clapping loudly.

Cecilia could feel the heat rising up her chest, closing in on her throat and coating her face. She could hear Jody calling her name from several rows behind her. "Cecilia, you owe me dinner and a movie!"

Flabbergasted, she adjusted her cap as she made her way to the stage.

"Congratulations, Miss Evans."

Cecilia could no longer hear the crowd. Time stopped as she stood before Judd.

She found a place of refuge in his dark eyes and was captivated by his smile as he pinned the ribbon on her gown and placed the envelope in her hand.

He turned toward the microphone and announced, "Miss Evans will now deliver the valedictorian speech for this graduating class."

The crowd clapped as Cecilia took her place at the podium. "Good morning, everyone. Thank you, Professor Taylor," she said, trying to compose herself enough to speak. "It is my honor to speak on behalf of the 2015 class of the McCombs School of Business at the University of Texas here in Austin." Before she could say anything else, her scanning eyes locked with his. There in the bleachers stood Daddy with his hand up.

Oh my god, is he going to say something? She rubbed the sweat from the back of her neck. *Is he going to ruin this for me right now? All that I've worked for to end like this.*

Daddy sat down when he was sure she had seen him.

Cecilia paused and turned toward Judd. "May I please have some water?"

She took the water he offered and slowly swallowed a few sips. *Daddy **will not** wreck this moment—I **will not** allow it!*

Cecilia turned her attention to the back of the auditorium and continued to speak, ending her speech with an admonition that nothing is too difficult if you work hard and stay focused on your dreams and goals.

The crowd stood, clapping and cheering. She laid the microphone on the podium, walked off the stage, and returned to her seat.

She sat motionless as the keynote speaker was introduced and stood to give his speech. Afterward, she heard nothing but applause. All she could think about was Daddy standing in the bleachers while everyone was seated so she could see him. *Why is he here? How did he get here?*

"Will the class of 2015 now rise?"

Now, it was time for her to stand and walk across the stage and receive the diploma she had spent almost every waking hour working for over the last four years. When she reached for that rolled-up piece of paper, she heard someone yelling, "Way to go, Cece! You did it!"

"Josh? Oh, my god, Josh *and* Daddy!" she said aloud as the president smiled, shook her hand and said, "Congratulations." *Did Mama and Ana come too?* She retook her seat and closed her eyes to keep the room from spinning. *Oh, my god, I'm scared. This can't be good. Nothing ever turns out good when Daddy's around.*

Cecilia was jarred back to reality when her class stood and began throwing their caps up, leading to the procession out of the auditorium.

"Cece!" Jody called as she ran up and hugged her tightly. "I'm so proud of you. I saw you getting choked up, and I got a little scared you might lose it, but you didn't! Your speech was perfect! And 1st prize *and* fifteen thousand dollars! You and Sophia beat out all those city artists!!! Wow, girl!"

"Hey Jody, my family's here," Cecilia interrupted, trying to warn her when she saw them approaching her.

"Your family?! I didn't think they were able to come."

"I didn't either," Cecilia said, staring Josh down.

"Cece!" He grabbed her up in a big bear hug and swung her around. "What just happened up there on that stage? We wanted to surprise you, but you took the prize, literally!" Josh said with a big grin. "Did you think for one hot minute that we wouldn't be here for your graduation from college? Cece! You're the only one in the family that's ever graduated from a four-year university! We just didn't know you were at the top of your class and gonna be speaking. We're the shocked ones! And the first-place winner of a big art contest that sold for fifteen thousand dollars What the heck?"

"Aren't you gonna properly introduce us, Cecilia?" Mama chimed in.

"Why didn't you tell me you were coming?"

"I should have, but Josh said not to."

"I'm sorry. Jody, this is my mama, Elizabeth, my daddy, Jim, my brother, Josh, and his wife, Ana. Jody's been my roommate and best friend for the last four years."

About that time, Jody's parents found them. "And this is my mother and father, Colleen and Jeff Hines. We're from North Carolina, too. Mom and Dad meet Cecilia's parents, Elizabeth and Jim Evans, and her brother Josh and his wife, Ana. They surprised her today!"

"Well, what a wonderful surprise!" Mrs. Hines said. "You must all be so proud of Cecilia."

"We are!" Mama said. "We didn't even know she could paint, and here she went and won first prize in an art contest and all that money. I sure hope we get to see that famous picture!"

There's a lot you don't know about me, Mama.

Daddy shook Mr. Hines's hand but remained quiet.

Cecilia was on such high alert for an imminent bomb dropping that she almost fell backward into Judd when he came up behind her.

"Hey, I was hoping to catch up with you before you left," Judd said, sounding out of breath. "I'm sorry I startled you."

"Judd, I mean Professor Taylor, my family surprised me," Cecilia said as she fumbled through the introductions again.

All eyes were on Judd as they watched Cecilia try to regain her composure.

"Everyone, this is Mr. Taylor, our art therapy professor."

Judd reached out and shook hands with everyone while Jody and Cecilia gave each other the eye.

"Just call me Judd. School's out now," he said, eyes glued to Cecilia. "Congratulations, again! Highest honors, first prize, and fifteen thousand dollars from the highest bidder. I guess you figured out the envelope I handed you was empty. We didn't want you walking around town with all that money. A check will be at the business office next week."

Cecilia could feel her face turning red. Still having difficulty accepting compliments, she whispered, "Thank you." She wanted to ask more questions about the auction but decided to wait, hoping to divert the attention away from herself since all eyes appeared to be staring at them.

"Would anyone like to grab some lunch? You guys are all on Eastern Standard Time, so you're probably getting hungry. I'd love to introduce you to Texas beef barbecue." She focused on Mama to avoid making eye contact with Daddy.

"You know there's only one kind of barbecue, Cece," Josh piped in.

"Yes, I know, you Tar Heels think real barbecue is pork! But, when in Texas!"

"Well, I think we should try it," Daddy said.

Who are you, and what have you done with Daddy?

"Mr. and Mrs. Hines, Jody, would you like to come with us?"

Cecilia asked, feeling more obligated to ask than really wanting them to come. Daddy always had a way of embarrassing her and ruining every special moment in her life.

"We'll have to pass this time," Mr. Hines answered. "We have some more family we're meeting. It was so nice to meet you folks, though, and I'm sure this won't be the last time."

Mrs. Hines hugged Cecilia and whispered, "Way to go, Cecilia."

"Thank you, Mrs. Hines, for all you did for me yesterday. I won't ever forget it."

"Love you, girl," Jody said as she leaned in closer for a hug and spoke in her ear, "Judd? I mean, Professor Taylor? You crack me up."

"Ha ha!"

"Mr. Taylor, thank you for teaching Jody. Whenever she called home this last semester, your class was the only one she ever talked about," Mr. Hines said.

"It was my pleasure. Jody is an extraordinary young lady. I love her honesty, and she added a lot to the class. She's quite talented."

"Yes, she is honest, brutally honest," Mrs. Hines said with a laugh. "Well, we had better get going, but meeting all of you was so nice."

"Jody, I'll see you back at the dorm this afternoon," Cecilia said.

"IF YOU'RE LOOKING for the best barbecue brisket in Texas, then you better fall in line at Franklin Barbecue," Judd said with a slight smile.

"Judd, you're welcome to come with us," Josh added.

"Sure, I'd ..." Judd started before Cecilia interrupted.

"Oh, I'm sure Mr. Taylor has plans this afternoon."

"I... I do have plans, but thank you for inviting me," Judd said, clearly getting her message of not wanting him to tag along. "It was nice to meet all of you. I am confident that Cecilia will excel in law school and whatever she pursues in the future," he said, nodding at her with a look of admiration.

He paused for several seconds before touching her on the shoulder, sending electrical jolts up her spine. "If you have any problems at the business office, let me know."

"Thanks, I will," she said with every nerve in her body now firing. She leaned in a little closer, and the faint scent of his cologne only intensified her yearning to be with him.

She glanced away to quench the building desire and noticed Josh and Ana studying her.

Oh, my god, get away from me before I make a stupid mistake and love you. I have to focus if I'm ever going to finish law school, and every time I'm around you, it makes it much harder for me to say no. I'm sorry for lying about your plans today, but I can't take the chance of Daddy blowing up at lunch, either. You don't know what it's like.

"Congratulations again, Cecilia," he said as he slipped away into the crowd.

30

EVERYONE WAS QUIET as Judd disappeared into the crowd. Then their attention turned to Cecilia.

"Why are ya'll staring at me?"

"I think he wanted to come, Cece," Josh said with a mischievous smile.

"No, he had plans."

"Oh, he told you his plans?"

"Stop it, Josh."

"What?"

"You know what!" she said while punching him in the arm.

"Ouch! Okay, I get it! No more talk about Mr. Romeo. Now, let's get this show on the road. We've got some hungry people here! And one of us is eating for two!" he said, staring at Ana.

"What? Are you kidding me? When?" She thought Ana had put a little weight on around the middle. "That's great news! I'm so happy for you!"

"Well, we hope you can make it home for Thanksgiving because little Josh Jr. should be here, and he'll want to meet his Auntie Cece!"

"Auntie Cece! I like the sound of that! Come on, let's go. We need to get this mama and baby boy something to eat. I can drive your car and probably get us there faster than you!"

The ride there was buzzing with talk about the baby, Josh's new job, and the house they planned to buy. Daddy was quiet—too quiet.

The line was long, and the midday Texas sun was heating up. Cecilia had found a table for everyone while she and Josh stood in line to order. Josh twisted the cap off the Texas Lone Star beer the waitress had brought him and took several big guzzles.

"Hey, is Daddy gonna want to start drinking when he sees you with that beer?"

"Don't think so. He quit drinking about a month after you left home."

Cecilia stood in shock, trying to digest the news. "Really? I suppose I *was* the reason he couldn't stop. Glad I could help by leaving."

"He dared us not to say anything to you. I suppose he wanted to make sure it would stick, and maybe he hoped you would come home sometime and see for yourself. Why don't you talk to him about it?"

"Maybe I will. Maybe I'll talk to him about a lot of things."

With all this good news, why do I feel so sad? Soph, I wish you were here.

They returned to the table with Texas beef brisket, coleslaw, potato salad, jalapeño cheddar sausage, pulled pork, key lime pie, and bottled waters.

"This looks wonderful," Mama said.

"I got some pulled pork for you Tarheels who only like pork barbecue! I think that will change when you try this brisket!"

Josh jumped right in to try the beef brisket. "Let me see what all this big talk is about," he said, chewing a big mouthful and chasing it with beer. He didn't speak for several seconds.

"Well, let's hear it, Josh. Say it! It's the best dang barbecue you've ever eaten!"

"This is undoubtedly the best dang barbecue my taste buds have ever experienced!"

"Here, here! To the best dang barbecue ever," they all said in unison as they held their water bottles high.

Cecilia noticed that Daddy hadn't ordered any alcoholic drinks.

"Not thirsty, Daddy? There's nothing like an ice-cold beer on a hot Texas day," she said, as if trying to test his ability to abstain.

"Nah, I gave that up a while back."

"Why'd you do that, Daddy? Because *I* finally left?"

"I'm not here to fight with you, Cecilia."

"Why *are* you here, then?"

"That's enough, Cecilia!" Mama said. "This has been a long trip for us all, especially for Ana."

Daddy looked down at his black dress work boots and shuffled them back and forth in the dirt. He took his white handkerchief from his pocket and wiped the sweat running down his brow.

"You're right. Let's enjoy this amazing key lime pie. I wanna hear more about Josh Jr.," Cecilia said.

"I'm a little tired," Ana said, pulling her red hair up in a ponytail and wiping the sweat from her neck with a paper towel. "I'd like to go back to the hotel. Maybe we could meet for dinner," Ana said as she rubbed her stomach.

Cecilia felt the regret of her words sticking in her throat. *Why did I want to fight with him? They drove across the country to see me graduate, yet I wanted to spew all the evil thoughts I'd ever had of him out into the open for the world to hear. I haven't seen him for four years, and when I do, I want to fight.*

Another wave crashed over her.

"ECILIA, WHY DON'T you come to the hotel so we can all get in the pool while Ana naps?" Mama asked.

"Sure. Where are ya'll staying?"

"At a Marriott not too far from the campus," Josh piped in.

"Okay, drop me off at the dorm. I'm supposed to meet Jody there to say our final goodbyes. I'll grab my bathing suit and be over shortly."

"Maybe Professor Taylor will be through with his obligations and come with you," Josh teased.

"Joshua Evans, you're getting ready to be in some big trouble if you don't stop with that!"

"You know I love you, sis!" he said as he tossed her the keys. "You drive. There are too many lanes for me."

"Whatever!"

"I don't care *who* drives as long as the AC is turned on high," Ana chimed in a highly irritated voice.

Cecilia stared at Ana, wiping the sweat from her forehead with another paper towel. *I'm sorry, Ana. It must have been terrible being cramped in the car for three days with Mama and Daddy, and on top of that, being pregnant. I'm such a jerk! What is wrong with me?* She had noticed the way Mama doted over Ana. *Mama, do you ever wonder about the grandbaby you didn't want? Stop it, Cecilia Evans! Don't go there.*

"Hey, it might feel good to get in the pool for a while and do some easy stretching before your nap," Cecilia said, trying to show some concern as they all packed in the car.

"Maybe so, we'll see," she said, yawning.

"I might even get in that pool," Daddy said.

"Well, that would be something. I can't remember when you or I were in a pool!" Mama said.

Josh laughed.

Cecilia kept quiet, afraid of what she might say. *Every time he says anything, I feel this anger rising in me. They won't be here long. I'll pretend we're one happy family. I can do whatever it takes to maintain peace, as long as I know there's an end in sight.*

Cecilia pulled the car close to her dorm and got out, handing the keys back to Josh.

"I'll see you guys soon. Is there anything you'd like me to bring?" she asked.

"Nope, I'm going to the grocery store as soon as I drop them off at the hotel. There's a grill by the pool. I thought I'd get some charcoal and pick up some chicken to cook out tonight. How does that sound?" Josh asked.

"It'll sound much better when I've had a chance to digest all the brisket and potato salad!"

"You'll be ready to eat again after we swim in that pool awhile," Mama said.

Cecilia smiled and waved goodbye as she walked back to the dorm.

SHE OPENED THE door to find Jody holding a big box, and her side of the room cleared out.

"Mom and Dad are downstairs loading the car with the rest of the stuff," Jody said as she put the box down and embraced Cecilia with a hug that perpetuated an opened floodgate of tears from them both.

"Oh, girls!" Mrs. Hines said as she came back in. "I know this has to be hard. Change is always hard, even if it's necessary. Cecilia, you are welcome at our home anytime."

"Thank you, but I don't know what I'll do here without Jody."

"And I can't *even* imagine life without my Cece!"

"Here," Mrs. Hines said, handing them a box of tissues. "Blow your noses now, and let's not prolong the inevitable."

"Your mom's right. My family's waiting for me at the hotel. I'm so glad we had our shopping day and stayed at the fancy hotel so we could talk all night. Now hurry up and leave before I start boohooing again!"

"One more quick hug and I'm outta here. You better call me regularly, though. Do you hear me?"

"Yes, counselor! And the same goes for you!" Cecilia said, choking back the tears.

"Bye for now, Cece. We love you and are proud of your accomplishments these last four years. I can't wait till you girls are practicing law and ridding the world of injustice!" Mrs. Hines added.

Nodding in agreement, Cecilia closed the door behind them and sat on the bed, staring at Jody's now barren side. "Sophie, if everyone weren't here, I'd just crawl under the covers and cry myself to sleep! I guess I better wear my suit, get over there, and try not to be rude again! Oh yeah, I almost forgot to tell you. I'm gonna be an auntie. I didn't even get to tell Jody!"

Cecilia looked at her plant and remembered waking up in the hospital to find it on her windowsill. *My baby would be about six now.* Another tear found its way down her cheek. Mrs. Hines had left the yellow roses on her desk along with the card. Cecilia stared at the envelope, wiped her eyes, and put her swimsuit on.

32

EVERYONE WAS IN the pool by the time she got to the hotel, including Ana.

"Hey, get in here! The water's great!" Josh yelled as Cecilia opened the gate to go in.

"Yeah, come on in," Ana called.

The water must have revitalized her.

Daddy was sitting on the side of the pool with his feet dangling in the water while Mama swam around and gave him a splash now and then. A straw hat sat on his head cocked to the right, and his Hawaiian print shirt was left unbuttoned, exposing his gray hairy chest.

Cecilia stared at them. For once in her lifetime, everyone seemed to be getting along.

This must be some Twilight Zone episode. Any minute now, it's going to happen—it always does. Stay quiet! Let them talk. I'm not going to start any trouble. Trouble will find them, I'm sure of it!

Ana had come alive and couldn't stop talking about the house they were buying and how she was decorating the baby's nursery.

I feel so alone even though I'm with them. It was good I went away so they could all come together and be one happy family. He couldn't even say goodbye to me, yet here he is, acting like everything is fine and dandy! Well, it's not!

"Anybody ready for some barbecued chicken now?" Josh asked while climbing out of the pool.

"I guess so. It's gettin' kind of late," Mama said as she busied herself pulling stuff out of the grocery bags.

Cecilia cringed when she saw Mama putting the red checkered cloth on the picnic table. She thought back to the tablecloth at the Italian restaurant they had gone to after her abortion. The day her life was changed forever.

Josh had thought of everything: baked potatoes already cooked, salads, and a cooler full of drinks. Everyone was having a good time. They all sat around and ate while making small talk.

Why do I still want to fight? No, I want to cry. No. I want to scream, yell at them, and give them a piece of my mind. But I can't. I never could tell them anything. It was all about them. They didn't care.

Cecilia felt uneasy when she noticed Daddy staring at her. *What do you want? You make me sick! Do you realize that? I hate you!*

Daddy looked away and then back at her. "Cecilia, would you go for a walk with me?"

What? I guess you didn't read my mind because if so, you sure wouldn't wanna go on a walk with me. "Sure," she blurted out.

Daddy got up from the table, and she followed his lead. Her leg muscles tightened as she prepared to run if she needed to. They walked down the street until Daddy motioned at the bench on the sidewalk. "How bout we sit here for a while?"

"Okay," she said with a tremor in her voice.

Cecilia sat beside him as he began to speak. "I want you to know something, Cece."

It had been a long time since he had called her that.

"I know I've done some terrible things to you. I quit drinking when you left because I realized how much pain I had caused you and the rest of the family. I can't change how I acted, but I want you to know I'm sorry. Real sorry. When I came home from Vietnam, I was not the same person. I'm doing better now. I've been going to counseling at the VA Hospital, and it's been helpful. Will you try and find some way to forgive me, Cecilia?"

She sat there paralyzed, thinking about all the times he had abused her in the darkness of the night, how he had physically and mentally abused all of them.

"Do you think I can just forgive and forget all the terrible things you did to us because you stopped drinking, and are going to counseling? Now you think you're all righteous or something?" Cecilia could feel her body quivering. *I need to get away from you. All I want to do is run! Far, far away where you can't hurt me anymore.*

"I know you won't forget, but I hope you will come to forgive me someday if you can't now." Torment occupied his eyes. The same torment that she used to feel when he threatened her to be quiet.

He handed her an envelope. "I wanted to bring you something for graduation. I worked on fishing boats on the weekends after you left and made pretty good money. I've been saving it for your graduation. I'm proud of you, Cece. You've made something of yourself."

Cecilia opened the envelope and saw a check for forty thousand dollars.

I'm going to vomit!

"Do you think you can buy my forgiveness? I don't need your money. I'm not for sale," she said as she handed him back the envelope.

Daddy stood up and folded the envelope before tucking it in his pants pocket. "I *am* sorry, Cecilia. I'll hold on to this if you decide you'd like it. Your mother has something for you also. Please accept her gift. She's been working on it for a long time."

"Why wouldn't I accept *her* gift?" she asked, glaring at him. *It's yours that I don't want.*

"I'm sorry, Cecilia. I didn't come here to cause you trouble. We should probably head back to the pool."

That's a good idea. Why did I even agree to go on a walk with you?

"You're back! Come sit down. I've been waiting to give you something." Mama kissed her cheek and handed her the box wrapped in graduation paper. "Go ahead and open it!"

Cecilia tore into the paper and opened the box to find a beautiful quilt with Texas bluebonnets and North Carolina dogwood blooms. "Did you do this, Mama?"

"I did."

"It's beautiful. Thank you so much."

Mama looked at Cecilia through teary eyes and whispered, "Please forgive me. I love you."

With rampant emotions, Cecilia hugged Mama and whispered words she never thought she'd say. "I forgive you, Mama, and I hope you'll forgive me. I'm sorry for the pain I caused *you.*" Mama nodded her head yes as they continued to embrace one another.

Cecilia thought back to the night she came in and found Mama on the floor with her head bleeding and Daddy standing over her with his fist raised. *I suppose she was a victim herself, even though I never understood why she didn't protect us.*

Josh and Ana moved in and handed Cecilia another card. "We put a little money in there to help keep you supplied with Franklin barbecue while you're in law school," Josh said, causing everyone to laugh.

"Thank you. It means a lot that you came to my graduation."

Daddy remained silent.

The following day, Cecilia showed them around campus and her dorm room. She appreciated that they all seemed genuinely interested in the campus and where she had lived, yet there was little to no inquiry about *her life* there. She thought about all the excuses she made to stay away from them. *It seems odd. I haven't been home since leaving there, not even for Christmas. Yeah, I always had an excuse, but if the truth be known, it was him I couldn't stomach to see again. Why, all of a sudden, right before graduation, did I want them all to show up? Here they are, and now I'm ready for them to leave and take him far away from me. Why is he so concerned with me forgiving him now? Is his conscience bothering him?*

Josh interrupted her swirling thoughts.

"I hate to cut this short, sis, but we gotta get going in a few minutes. I wanna get out of the Austin traffic as soon as possible. I'm gonna drive as far as I can, and then we'll get a hotel room. Ana and I have work on Thursday, but we *all* wanted to come and celebrate with you."

Cecilia walked them to the car and watched as they drove away after many goodbyes.

If he stopped drinking a month after I left home, why didn't he call, write, or do something before now? No, he waited until my day and then made it about himself. He wanted something else from me, like usual. Did he think I would just forgive him and everything would be great like it seemed to be between all of them? Well, it's not great, Daddy. It's just not! Maybe you should have thought about getting help a lot sooner!

Back in the dorm, she wrapped herself up in the quilt, lay on her bed by the window, and stared at Sophia sitting proudly on the sill. "Sweet Soph, you've been with me every time life has tried to swallow me up. You deserved first prize! Your beauty will shine now for all to see when they look at your picture." Cecilia closed her eyes, hoping her mind could find some rest.

33

CECILIA STIRRED TO someone knocking on the door.
Fumbling her way out of bed, she heard the knock again.
"What time is it? Coming!"

"Cecilia, it's me, Judd."

"Judd, what are you doing here?" she asked, opening the door.

"Don't I even get a hello before you send me away?"

"Oh, I'm sorry. I must have fallen asleep," she said, straightening her clothes and pushing her hair behind her ears.

"I was just wondering if you'd like some ice cream?"

"Ice cream?"

"Yeah, ice cream."

"Okay. But this isn't a date or anything."

"No, just ice cream," he said, smiling like he had won the prize behind door number one.

"Let me grab a sweater."

She could feel his breath on her neck as he helped put her sweater on.

Cecilia moved quickly to the door and closed it behind them. *I won't be in my room alone with you, Judd Taylor! Do you think I'm crazy?*

Judd carried the conversation with great ease as they walked down the street to the ice cream shop. "How did your family like Franklin Barbecue?"

"They loved it! Even agreed it was the best dang barbecue they ever had."

"You know you can't go wrong with Franklin!"

"Thanks for the recommendation. Sorry I didn't ask you along. I was shocked they even came and wasn't sure how it would go. My dad and I have never gotten along well."

"I understand, Cecilia. You don't need to explain. I'm glad they were able to come and witness your achievements."

"Speaking of that. Who bought my artwork?"

"The buyer wanted to remain anonymous and had an agent for proxy bidding. They've had that happen before. There are many reasons buyers choose to stay anonymous. Sometimes it's for privacy or security, or maybe they buy the art as a gift."

"As long as the money gets in my account, it doesn't matter. Fifteen thousand dollars! That's unbelievable. Are you sure it's legit?"

"The City's Art Council knows what it's doing. Visit the business office on Monday and see for yourself."

"I believe I will."

"What kind of ice cream would you like?"

"Raspberry cheesecake, of course! Is there any other kind?"

"Coming right up."

Sitting at the outdoor table, they ate silently until Judd offered her some of his chocolate mocha while bringing his spoon close to her mouth. She opened her mouth and ate it to prevent him from dropping it on her.

"Well, you're one step closer to your dream," Judd said.

Her expression grew solemn. "Ahh, yeah. My dream. Law school."

"What's wrong?"

"For a moment, I'd forgotten about school, Jody and my family leaving, and why I can't be in a relationship with you right now."

"Hold on. Wait a minute. I don't like the sound of that."

"Judd, law school will be three long years at least, and they say the first year is the hardest. I'm going to have to stay focused. I can't just be friends with you because it would escalate quickly into something more. I'm sorry, Judd."

"I don't believe that's the only reason you won't give us a chance.

What is it, Cece? Talk to me. I'm tired of playing games. I care about you, and I know you care about me."

She stared blankly at him while thoughts of all her childhood nights and the abortion clinic invaded her soul.

He reached over to touch her arm. With a shiver, she tried to shake off the foreboding feeling slowly wrapping around her body.

Don't touch me! Memories of all the unwanted intruders crashed over her as she gasped for air.

"Judd, whatever it *was* is now over."

"Just like that?"

"Just like that. I'm sorry."

When she got up, her heart began to beat frantically in her chest. She threw the unfinished ice cream cone into the trash and walked down the street without looking back.

Keep moving, Cecilia, before you can't.

"JODY'S GONE—NO CALLS from Judd. Mama, Daddy, Josh, and Ana are back in North Carolina. And here I am. Do I expect him to call after such fierce rejection? Do I secretly want him to keep on groveling for my attention? No, it's over. I can't expect anything. It's not fair to ask him to wait for me. He needs someone that doesn't have so much baggage. I have to finish law school! I promised myself."

She looked at her shimmering plant. "I can always count on you. Thanks for listening, Sophie!"

The next couple of weeks before school started were spent on moving into an apartment across from the campus and thrifting for furniture, artwork, and whatever else she needed to make the new place homey.

"It's a good thing I don't own much. It sure has made move-in day a lot easier. Thanks to you, Soph, I got a new bed and frame from the artwork sale. They even delivered it and set it up for me. I'm gonna sleep well tonight in my very own bed!"

Her mind drifted back to the morning she woke in the hospital to see the plant on the windowsill, beaming as a ray of sunlight outlined her leaves. *He* had left it for her.

Who was he? Who would stay in the hospital all night sitting by the bedside of someone they didn't know? Did he know me? Why would he pay my bill? The same questions seemed to weigh on her year after year.

"I wish Jody had stayed here to attend law school with me. I guess she's busy too, Soph." Cecilia made some tacos and sat on the couch to eat them.

With her last bite, she grabbed her cell phone and called Jody's number.

"Hello, is this Reed and Dunbar's office?"

"Yes, it is; how may I help you?"

"Let's cut to the chase. Do I have to pay upfront for your services?"

"Yes, ma'am, you do!"

"Would a couple of tacos suffice as a retainer?"

"You crazy nut! I've missed you."

"Good! Come back!"

"Ha ha!"

"This is the first night in the apartment, and Sophie is tired of listening to me!"

"I miss you, Cece! You make me laugh!"

"Well, this won't make you laugh."

"What have you done?"

"I told Judd it was over."

Silence.

"Please don't be mad at me. I have to finish law school, and I wouldn't be able to focus with him around."

"Well, at least you finally admitted it."

"Admitted what?"

"You're in love with him, and you can't think of anything else when he's around! You can thank me again for forcing you into art therapy class! Not only did you finish with the best-looking guy on campus in love with you, but your picture of sacred Sophie won you a bundle! You need to take good care of that girl and don't talk her to death. She brings you good luck or something for sure!"

"She is amazing! If you ever tell anyone I talk to her, I'll plead the fifth!"

"Your secrets are good with me. I love and miss you, Cecilia Evans!"

152

Mom's calling, so I had better go, but I'll call you soon to see how school is going. And give Judd a chance, you silly girl!"

"Talk soon, friend."

35

CECILIA SAT WITH her eyes glued to the front of the room as the professor began to lecture. "The state of Texas reinstated capital punishment in 1976. One-fourth of your grade this semester will culminate with a debate on the pros and cons of the death penalty."

"You know you wanna do this, Miss Summa Cum Laude."

Cecilia turned around to see a taunting grin on Brett McCain's familiar face. The ladies' man had always been surrounded by an entourage of circling female piranhas in the few undergrad classes they had shared.

"Matter of fact, I do."

The professor wrote FOR/PROS CAPITAL PUNISHMENT on the left side of the whiteboard and AGAINST/CONS CAPITAL PUNISHMENT on the right side.

"I'd like you to come up to the board and write your full name on the side you wish to debate."

Brett stood first, holding his hand out for her to go before him.

This should be interesting. Picking up the marker, Cecilia went to the left side of the board and, without hesitation, wrote her name under the FOR column.

All but four followed Brett as they went to the right and wrote their names.

"Miss Evans, I'd like you to be the chair of your team and Mr.

McCain the chair of yours since you two were the first to respond. Here are the guidelines," Professor Greene said, as he handed the list to each of them.

Cecilia mingled with the others on her team. "Well, everyone, we may be the underdog." Everyone laughed while she handed them her notebook to get their names and phone numbers.

Cecilia glanced at Brett to see several female students listening intently to every word he said.

I can't wait to tell Jody who I'm up against. Or who he's up against.

"Cecilia, wait a minute," Brett called as she walked out the door.

"Yeah?"

"Don't you think we should get together and review these guidelines so we'll be on the same page?"

"I guess so. I figured *they* would tell you how to run the show," she said sarcastically as the girls from his team walked by, giving him the eye.

"What?"

Cecilia blushed and wished she hadn't spoken what was on her mind so freely. "I'll meet you in the library tomorrow afternoon at four," she said ignoring his question.

"I can do that."

"See you then," she said as she hurried down the steps to avoid further conversation.

CECILIA COULD HARDLY wait to get inside her apartment to call Jody.

"Hey, you will *never* believe the day I've had."

"Do tell!"

"Guess who I will be debating in Professor Greene's class?"

"Come on, Cecilia, who?"

"Brett McCain!"

"What?"

"You heard me. We are team leaders for the great debate our class will be doing on the pros and cons of capital punishment."

"Well, that should be interesting! You better beware of him, Cece.

From the stories I've heard about him, he's a sleazeball. His dad is some fancy lawyer downtown, and he's a shark who takes on big clients and always seems to win."

"Now, Jody, are you trying to lead the witness?"

"I'm just saying, be careful around him. He's not Judd."

Cecilia got quiet.

No, he's not. There's no one like Judd.

"Cece, do you hear me?"

"Yeah, I hear you."

"Sorry to be the downer. Work the debate and keep it at that."

"I will."

"Okay, good."

"I'm gonna go take a bubble bath and tell Soph about my day now!"

"Love you, friend."

"Love you more. Bye."

36

"OH, MY GOD, I'm gonna be late. I hate being late. Brett better not say a word about it either." Cecilia turned the corner in the library and found him at a table with three other guys she had never seen before.

"Hey," she said, appearing to be breaking up some lively conversation.

"I'm glad you could make it," he said, getting up and steering her to another, more private table. "How have you been?" he asked while pulling the chair out for her.

"You mean since yesterday?"

"Yeah."

Cecilia rolled her eyes as she thought of Jody calling him a sleazeball.

"I'm kinda getting the vibe you don't like me," he said.

"This isn't about me liking you or not. This is about how we're going to run the debate."

"Whoa. I'm not sure I'd like to be up against you in a courtroom."

Cecilia cracked a smile, and the tension seemed to dissipate somewhat.

She wasted no time. "Alright, this is what I'm thinking. Our job will be to formulate the questions to be debated. We'll call one person up to the podium at a time. You and I will take turns presenting questions and they will speak based on the research they've done. They will be timed. What do you think?"

"I can see why you were Miss Summa Cum Laude. You're quite the take charge, get it done kind of person."

"Thank you, I guess, *if* you meant that as a compliment."

"How else would I mean it?"

Something about him just didn't sit right with her. "I need to get home now."

"Wait, would you like to get something to eat?"

Cecilia stood still, not sure how to respond to his unexpected invitation.

"Aren't you hungry? We could brainstorm and solve some of these questions. I can tell you're not a procrastinator!"

Cecilia stared into his eyes, trying to read him.

"Okay."

Yeah, the sooner we get this over with, the better.

"Okay, then," he repeated.

"Yes, but I can't stay late. I'm working on a paper that's due soon."

"I know this Thai restaurant that's not too far."

"That's fine," Cecilia said as she gathered her things and got up.

The walk there was dreamlike. Cecilia hadn't walked anywhere with a man except Judd since she had moved to Austin. Looking around, it seemed everyone was a couple, something she had never noticed.

Brett held the door open for her as they entered the packed restaurant.

"Two for dinner?" the hostess asked.

"Yes," they both said in unison.

"It will be a while before a table is available, but you can sit at the bar. You may order and eat there if you like. It'll probably be faster."

"That'll be fine," Cecilia answered before Brett could reply.

The hostess handed them menus. Brett took Cecilia's free hand and guided her as he wove between the crowd to reach the bar. He helped her onto a barstool and sat down beside her. The last man to take her hand was Judd.

Beware of him, Jody had warned.

Cecilia had already begun to study the menu when the bartender approached them, asking for a drink order.

"I'll have a draft beer," Brett said without hesitation.

Taking a napkin, Cecilia wiped the sweat from her hands.

"I'll have a house margarita on the rocks," she said without looking up.

"You've got it," he said as he turned and immediately opened the tap to fill Brett's mug with beer.

I'm gonna need something stronger than tea to get through this meeting. Why did I agree to go to dinner with him? And drinks? Am I crazy? Jody told me to beware of him. Is he the sleazeball she said he was?

"Thank you," she said as the bartender placed an oversized margarita in front of her and asked if she needed anything else.

Did he know I'd need a stiff drink to get through this time with Brett? Maybe Brett was a regular, and he knew what kind of guy he was.

"I can't believe we never got together in undergrad, but here we are now," he said as he lifted his mug for a toast. "Here, here, to the great debate!"

Cecilia used both hands to lift the massive glass to her lips and sip the tart margarita.

She continued to take more sips while Brett went on and on about himself.

"Yeah, my father's already promised to make me partner as soon as I pass the bar exam."

"It must be nice to have everything planned out for you like that."

"What? You think my father's giving me everything on a silver spoon?" he asked while catching the bartender's attention.

"I didn't say that."

"Bring me a shot; no, make it a double of whiskey, will you? And bring the lady here another margarita."

Cecilia didn't object, seeing she had struck a raw nerve. *One mention of his father, and he turned from Jekyll to Hyde!*

"We better get to business here," she said. "It's getting late."

"Oh yeah, right. What would you like to eat?" Brett motioned for the waitress.

"Are you ready to order now?"

"Cecilia?"

She stared at the menu for a few seconds, then closed it and laid it on the table. "I'll have some chicken pad thai."

"And I'll have the shrimp pad thai."

"Will that be all?"

"Yes, ma'am," he replied after seeing Cecilia nod yes.

The bartender returned with the drinks right as the waitress was leaving.

Cecilia stared at Brett as he downed the double shots of whiskey and nodded at the bartender to bring him another round.

Her anxiety climbed to a new level as Brett stood up and handed her the margarita and then bent over to kiss her on the forehead.

"No thanks, I've had enough."

Ignoring her, he sat back down and downed the next round the bartender had dropped off.

"Do two wrongs make a right?" he mumbled as he stared straight ahead.

"What are you talking about?"

He turned toward her, and his glassy eyes cut her to the quick.

"You know, capital punishment. Wouldn't it be more punishment for someone to rot in prison? And besides, what if the person is tried and convicted wrongly? What then? We put to death an innocent man. Aren't we then guilty of murder? There have been cases. How do we know what is truth?"

"Are you kidding me? The evidence tells the truth, Brett! The evidence doesn't lie. That's why we have put ourselves through this torture all these years! So we can now figure out the truth." She could feel her blood boil as she raised the fresh margarita to her lips.

Brett raised his eyebrows as Cecilia ranted about truth and justice.

She could see Brett was getting excited just listening to her defense. He stood again and whispered in her ear. "Hey baby, you're turning me on!"

"Oh, my god, you're sick!"

"Do you like sick?" he asked as he drew her close and forced his tongue down her throat until she gagged.

"No!!" she shouted while pulling away. "You're not only sick, you're drunk! And don't ever call me baby!" she yelled over the noise in the bar as she stormed out.

"May the best lawyer win!" he shouted behind her.

The bartender quickly made his way over to Brett.

"Hey buddy, it looks like that whiskey's gone to your head. Do you want me to call you a cab because you'll need to leave?"

"I don't need a cab!" he yelled as he pulled out a hundred-dollar bill, threw it on the bar, and proceeded to stagger toward the door. "No one turns me down! Who does that bitch think she is?"

Cecilia ran back to her apartment, afraid to look back to see if he had followed her. With trembling hands, she unlocked the door, quickly shut, and relocked it.

"He's not just a sleazeball, he's crazy! Why didn't I listen to you, Jody? I need Sophie!" She went to her bedroom and ran the tub full of warm water. She placed Soph on the tub's edge, undressed, and stepped in. "Oh, Soph, I can't believe that slimeball put his tongue in my mouth!" Holding her breath, she submerged her head under the water and then came up for air, shaking her head as if trying to wash all the yuck of the night away.

"He can come up with his questions! And *yes, sir*, may the best lawyer win!"

37

BRETT HAD LIT a fire in Cecilia that was now raging.

How dare he call me baby! And he had the nerve to make a move on me right there at the bar! He doesn't know who he's messed with. I don't care if he was drunk. I'm not just another one of his groupies! I dare you to put your hands on me again, Mr. Brett McCain.

She looked forward to the next class with him, hoping he might say something he'd regret.

Arriving at class, she sat in her regular seat.

I refuse to let him intimidate me, she thought as she plopped her book on the desk behind him loud enough to make him jump.

"Hey, Cecilia. I was hoping we might have a chance to talk before class started."

"Really?"

"Yes. I need to apologize to you for how I acted the other night. I'm sorry and want ya to know that will never happen again. You can trust me. Something triggered me when you commented on everything working out for me. My father seems to have my whole life planned, and I'm not sure if it's the life I want. I'm sorry for the way I treated you."

Not expecting to see him groveling, as he seemed to be doing, Cecilia felt like water had been thrown on her fire.

"I appreciate your explanation."

"Truce then?" he asked.

Cecilia stared at him, trying to detect what was the *truth*.

"How bout we just try to be civil to one another while in this class?"

"Civil it is! Let's work with our groups and start this debate."

Professor Greene arrived and instructed the class to turn to page 225 in their textbooks. He reminded them to continue working on the debate, as it would be a significant part of their final grade.

Brett turned around and winked at Cecilia. "I know you like all A's."

"Yes, I do, Mr. McCain, and I have worked very hard for every *A* I've gotten," she responded, testing his reaction.

Despite holding his tongue, he couldn't stop the heat rising up his neck and making his face smolder.

"You okay, Mr. McCain?"

"Just fine, Miss Evans," he said with a calculating smile. "Let's do this."

"You're on," she responded, feeling like she had just won.

"May the best lawyer win!" he said, suddenly sure of himself.

"You seem to use that statement a lot, Mr. McCain," she responded, remembering the night he yelled those exact words as she left the restaurant.

He started to say something but got quiet as one of the girls from his group sat beside him and started talking.

Time will tell, she thought.

Spurred on to see it happen, Cecilia arranged all the meeting times in the library as the groups researched their questions and prepared to discuss the pros and cons of the death penalty in Texas. A genuine camaraderie was formed within each group as they passionately shared their voices.

Cecilia stayed civil with Brett but remained guarded, believing him a timebomb that might explode with the least amount of friction. Whenever she felt her resistance toward him lessen, she reminded herself of the night at the Thai restaurant.

"Hey, Cecilia," Brett said one night after everyone had left the library. "I'd like the teams to come to my house this Friday night. I thought we could have some Chinese food together and have a practice debate. We could all dress for court. What do ya think?"

The last time dinner didn't turn out well at all, but this would be a group thing, and he hadn't made any moves or done anything inappropriate since that night.

"What time are you thinking?" she answered.

"How about seven? I'll send an email out since everyone's gone."

"Alright, I'll see ya later."

Cecilia could feel her defenses going out the window. *Have I been wrong about him?*

That night, she retrieved the black dress and red heels from her closet that Mrs. Hines had bought her on their shopping spree before graduation.

"This should work, or should I say it's court-approved? What do you think, Soph? Are the red shoes a little too much? Too bad. I will be wearing them, and I approve!"

FRIDAY NIGHT CAME. Cecilia curled her hair and shaved her legs. "Girl, you are looking fine tonight!" she said, slipping into the reserved black dress. She put her hose on and glided her feet into the magical red slippers. "I feel good about tonight. It's time to shine for the cause!"

She decided to walk to Brett's place since it wasn't too far. With a quick knock on the door, he answered. "Hey, you're the first to arrive, but I wouldn't expect anything less from Miss Summa Cum Laude."

Cecilia gave a short laugh even though something felt odd.

"Come on in. The guys here are just finishing up a poker game."

"Would you like something to drink?"

"A Coke would be fine."

Brett returned with her drink and assured her everyone would be there soon.

Cigar smoke lingered as the guys continued to place their bets. Cecilia tried to cough to clear her throat.

"Hey everyone, do you remember Cecilia? Miss Suma Cum Laude?"

Why does he always call me that?

The guys looked up, holding their beer bottles like they were toasting.

Feeling uneasy, she drank her Coke and handed Brett the glass.

"I remember you. Weren't you all in the library when I first met with Brett?" Cecilia asked.

A burst of laughter made her jump.

"That was us!"

She noticed her vision was getting blurry as she saw everyone throwing more money on the table and passing the cards out. She could hear Brett taking bids and saw him collecting money.

"Cecilia, *you* are the guest of honor tonight, and you look hot."

"I'm not feeling so well," she said as she clung to his arm. "When's everyone coming?"

"Oh, I forgot to tell you. They're not. I thought we'd have our own private debate. Us," he continued as he pointed to the guys, "against you."

Cecilia tried to reach the door, but Brett stepped before her, blocking the way.

"What's going on?" she asked as he picked her up and carried her down the hall. The look in his eyes scared her as she struggled to get away. "Please, no," she muttered.

"Don't talk!" he said while throwing her on the bed. She could hear the men's voices mocking her.

"Please, I'm begging you, Brett."

"Keep begging, Miss Suma Cum Laude, but it won't help," he said with a crazed and evil look in his eyes. "There will be no evidence to tell the truth. I guess you're not as good as you thought you were. Now shut up!"

Her fight was gone. Both arms and legs were limp. Unable to move, she saw the blurry outlines of the guys standing over her, taking their pants off. She wanted to scream as she felt herself falling into the deep, dark, bottomless pit of hell. *Why me?*

38

CECILIA WOKE EARLY the following day on her bed, still dressed in the clothes she had worn the night before. *Oh god, this wasn't a bad dream. It was a living nightmare. How did I get home?* Her head pounded as the last thing she remembered was them standing over her, taking their pants off and laughing as she begged them *not* to.

I need some water. I'm so dizzy. Grabbing hold of the dresser, she stood up and waited until her balance returned before going down the hall to the kitchen. There on the bar were her keys. With her head now on fire, she stumbled and dropped to the floor. The coolness of the tile felt good to the pulsating veins in her head.

"What *did* they do to me?"

As she pulled her legs in closer to her chest, a sharp pain in her abdomen made her stretch them out again. Groans escaped through her closed mouth. Struggling for breath, she forced the words out that she had dared not say before in case he was real. "God, I hate…God, I hate y…No, I hate myself. I was so stupid to fall for his trick. This is my fault. Yeah, I screwed up. I own my mistakes. But you, God, *you* could have stopped them. Jody's a Christian. She said you see every-thing. How *could you* watch what they did to me and not stop them? Why didn't you just let them kill me? I can't do this anymore."

Cecilia pulled herself up and slowly crept to the bathroom, leaving a trail of clothes behind. She used what strength she could muster to undress along the way. Turning the heat up, she stepped into the shower and let the scalding water seer her body, leaving every inch of her skin bright red. "I'm so dirty!" she cried, sliding down the side of the shower wall. She sat there sobbing long enough for the hot water to turn cold.

Cecilia remained sitting, shivering as the now freezing water pulsated over her body.

"You won, you sleazeball. I played right into your hands," she cried, choking on every word. Standing to her feet, she pulled the towel from the rack and dried off.

She found her jogging pants and a sweatshirt from her dresser and pulled them onto her damp body.

Grabbing a trash bag from the kitchen drawer, she stuffed it with the clothes strewn across the floor and made her way to the dumpster behind her apartment.

"Trash," she said as she dropped the bag in.

Are you crazy? You just threw away the evidence. Don't you want to see them pay for what they did to you?

"Shut up," she gasped, as the stabbing pain in her belly caused her to stop and bend over. *I have to get back indoors.* She wiped the tears from her eyes on her sleeve and stood up, putting one foot in front of the other until she made it back into her apartment. Pushing the door shut, she locked it and went to the bathroom.

"Who are you?" she said as she stared into the mirror. "What am I supposed to do with this mess? Did I think things would be better here in Austin than in North Carolina? Was I doomed from birth to be abused, or am I just getting what I deserve for having the abortion?" Cecilia opened the medicine cabinet and reached for the sleeping pills she had gotten from the clinic for her insomnia. "I'm tired…tired of it all. I just want to go to sleep and never wake up." She filled a glass with water and went to the living room. Turning on the television, she remembered how Daddy blared the TV so loudly that no one could hear anything else.

"Daddy, is this loud enough for you?" She turned the volume on the remote as high as it would go. "Maybe you wanted to drown out the noises in your head like I do now." Pouring the pills out on the coffee table where Sophia was sitting, she began to swallow them until they were all gone. "Soph, maybe someone will plant you in a beautiful garden one day where you belong." Lying on the couch, she covered up in the quilt Mama had made her for graduation. "Oh, Jody, I hope someone gives you this quilt. *You* were the best friend I ever had."

"Mama, I'm sorry. I'd leave you a note, but I don't know what to say. Josh and Ana, I'm sorry I'll never get a chance to meet Josh Jr. Jo… dy." She could feel her eyes getting heavy.

She thought she heard the phone ringing. *I can't talk. Mama, no one can hurt me anymore.* A loud banging on the door persisted. *Who's there? Go away. I can't fight anymore. All those years of trying to be the best at everything. For what? I'm so tired.*

"Her TV's been rocking my floor. I knocked on the door to ask her to turn it down, but she didn't answer. I've never heard any noise coming from her apartment before," Cecilia's neighbor reported to the apartment manager.

The apartment manager banged on her door when no one answered the bell. "I'm gonna open the door now," he yelled.

"Oh God," the neighbor said as they found her on the couch, unresponsive, with the empty pill bottle on the table beside her. "Call 911!"

"There's a young woman in the apartments across from the UT campus at 1301 Ridgewood Drive, apartment 101A, that appears to be a suicide attempt."

"Is she breathing?"

"Yes."

"Can you feel her pulse?"

"Yes, but it's weak."

"An ambulance is close by and will be there within minutes."

Is this what it feels like to die? Swirling like a tornado sucking me into its tunnel. Why couldn't I just go to sleep and never wake up? Did I screw this up too? Go away!

"They're here now," the apartment manager reported to the person who answered the 911 call.

Cecilia shivered as the medic placed a cold stethoscope on her chest. With his other hand, he grabbed her wrist, feeling for a pulse.

Am I dying? I can't move. Who's talking?

"Her pulse is weak, and her breathing is shallow," the medic said as he placed an oxygen mask on her face. "Let's get her on this stretcher and into the ambulance now."

His voice commanded attention, and with a flurry of activity, Cecilia was on the stretcher and attached to a monitor.

Wait, leave me.

"Come on now. Let's get moving. Time matters. Steve, grab her purse on the table there so we can have some ID."

He took Cecilia's hand and squeezed it tightly. "This is not the end, young lady. Whatever caused you to do this is not worth taking your life for. You fight. You hear me?"

She made a weak attempt to squeeze his hand back. *I'm so tired.*

"Man," the medic said to the neighbor on the way out the door, "you probably just saved her life."

Judd was outside on campus walking when he heard sirens going off. He had made an effort to walk by her apartment on the way to class in hopes of a chance to see her. Jody had secretly given him her address. He went across the street and saw someone rolled out on a stretcher to the ambulance.

"Oh, my God! Cecilia? Hey, what happened here? I know this young woman. She was a student of mine."

"Do you know anyone to call for her, perhaps her family?" the medic asked.

"No, I don't know how to reach them right now, but I'll try and find out. May I ride with her? Her name is Cecilia Evans."

"Okay, sit here in the back."

Judd didn't take his eyes off her.

Pale and barely breathing, she thought she heard him pray. "Please, God, save her. Please save her! Cece, it's me, Judd. I'm here, and I'm not going to leave you. Hang in there, Cece. Don't you die on me! Do you hear me?"

Judd…

"Cece, I'm here. Stay with us."

"Sir, we need you to stay seated while we start this IV."

Cecilia squinted as a bright light summoned her. In the distance, she saw Brett and his chums, all dressed in black, making their way toward her. The smoke of cheap cigars filtered out from their nostrils. She gasped for air, making every breath a struggle. The darkness was invading her light.

"Help me," she whimpered while trying to rise.

"Cece, it's okay. I'm here," Judd said as he choked, trying to get the words out. "Oh, my God, I can't stand to see her like this. Help her, God."

Pulling into the ER circle, the ambulance stopped, and someone opened the door from the outside. A team of staff members were awaiting her arrival, and everyone acted fast to get her inside. He saw the empty bottle of sleeping pills the medic handed the nurse.

"Hey, someone talk to me! I need to stay with her." Invisible and helpless, he watched as they rolled her away.

"Sir, are you family?" a nearby ER nurse asked.

"No, I'm her…I'm a friend. She doesn't have any family here."

"You'll have to wait in the waiting room. Someone will talk to you as soon as they can."

"Alright."

"Come with me. I'll show you where it is. Are you okay?" she asked.

"I'm okay. It's Cecilia I'm worried about."

She returned with a cup of cold water. "Here, drink this, and if you need anything, go to the desk."

"I will. Thank you."

Why, Cecilia? Why would you do something like this? Judd took a seat in the waiting room. *Please, God, save her.*

He sat staring at the television, blinded by emotion. The hands on the large clock above the ER doors continued to move as he sat waiting and wringing his hands.

The room bustled with people coming in and out, but he was deaf to everything around him until someone called his name.

"Judd, is that you?" asked a young man in scrubs approaching him. "Are you with the young woman they brought in?"

"Mike, thank God it's you. I didn't know you worked here! Yeah, I know her. She was a student of mine and a friend. How is she?"

"Well, she's lucky. She probably wouldn't have made it if the neighbor hadn't called. She'd taken enough pills to never wake up again."

Feeling nauseous at the news, Judd sat down. "May I see her, Mike?"

"Yeah, I'll give you a few minutes with her. She's stable right now and starting to wake up a little. See if she'll talk to you. Find out what you can and if there's anyone she'd like for us to call."

"I will. Hey, thanks, Mike," Judd said as he got up and shook his hand.

"Come on, I'll take you to her."

Mike pulled the curtain back. "Cecilia, someone's here to see you."

Cecilia stared at the wall in a near-catatonic state.

Mike looked at Judd and patted his shoulder. "I'll leave you two alone for a minute."

"Thanks, Mike."

Judd walked around the bed, choking back the tears. Her ghostly white face appeared lifeless.

"Oh, my God, Cece!" He wiped his eyes on his sleeve and slid her hand into his.

She pulled away and squeezed her eyes shut. Shaking her head from side to side, her body trembled. She could smell the stale cigar smoke and began to moan as the shaking became more violent.

"Cecilia, it's me, Judd. You're safe. I'm here, and I won't let anyone hurt you."

He pulled her in closer to his chest with his arms embracing her.

"Why?" she whispered. She could see the faint outline of their faces. "What do you want from me? Somebody, help me."

"Cece, I'm here. It's Judd."

"Why me?" she cried.

"Open your eyes, Cece. You're in the hospital, and you're safe. I've got you. You're going to get through this. You have to."

She opened her eyes to find herself embraced in Judd's arms.

"That's good, Cece, stay with me."

"I don't want to get through this," she said as she stared at him with lost eyes.

"Shhh. Just rest now."

He helped her to lay back and watched as her eyes fell shut again.

The color was slowly returning to her face as he pulled the blanket around her shoulders and kissed her gently on the cheek.

"Be still, Cece. I'm right here. I love you," he whispered.

39

CECILIA STIRRED AND opened her eyes when the doctor returned. "Cecilia, I'm Dr. Denton. Mike Denton," he said as he looked at Judd. "Do you have any family here?"

"No."

"Would you like us to call a family member for you?"

Cecilia shook her head no and looked at Judd.

"Would you like your friend to step outside while we talk?"

"No, he can stay."

"You gave us quite the scare. You probably wouldn't be with us if the neighbor hadn't called for help. Will you tell me what happened?"

"I've been in school for a long time. I guess just dealing with school and finances got the best of me. I've been overwhelmed lately," she said softly.

Cecilia glanced at Judd to see if he was buying her alibi.

Judd remained quiet.

"Have you ever done anything like this before?"

"No."

Mike continued asking her questions, and to Judd's amazement, Cecilia shot back appropriate answers every time.

"What you did was very serious, and we need to know you are safe. Do you feel safe?"

"I don't know." *Will I ever feel safe again?*

"I'd like to transfer you to Oak Ridge Psychiatric Hospital for more evaluation. You will have a chance to meet with counselors who can help you with coping skills."

Cecilia, too weak to argue, nodded her head yes.

"We'll send you by ambulance. Do you have any questions for me?"

"No."

Mike nodded at Judd and exited the room.

"I'm cold," she mumbled, shivering.

Judd retrieved a blanket from the closet and draped it over her.

"Thanks," she said faintly.

He started to say something, but Cecilia interrupted.

"It's okay. I'll be okay," she said, trying to relieve the fear in his eyes.

"Is it? Is *it* okay, Cecilia?" he asked while touching her arm.

She pulled away and turned over to escape his look.

"Hey, what's going on?" he asked. "I wanna be here for you, but you keep pushing me away."

She remained silent.

"Cecilia, I'm here to listen and help you. Just *let* me know how."

God, I'm so embarrassed. Why did he have to see me like this? I've done nothing but reject him and cause him pain. I'm so not worth his love!

"Judd, it's complicated."

"Knock, knock," a nurse said as she entered the room. "Cecilia, the transport team will be here in a few minutes, and the police would like to ask you a few questions."

Cecilia motioned for Judd to leave.

"I'll be right outside," he said, nodding as he passed the nurse.

"Judd, please, just *go*."

He hesitated a moment.

"Judd?"

He turned, hope plastered on his face.

"Nothing."

"My number hasn't changed," he said.

"Judd, please don't tell anyone, especially Jody."

Oh God, why did he have to see me like this? I wanted to go to sleep and never wake up.

A flurry of activity continued as the police entered. After they left her room, the transport team arrived.

"Are you ready to go?" asked one of the nurses.

"Yes."

AND I THOUGHT trashing RJM's painting would get me put away.
Her heart began to beat faster when the medic announced they would be arriving any minute now. *Oak Ridge Psychiatric Hospital, are you kidding me? Was this my intended destiny all along? Okay, I need to act cool and get out of this place. How will I ever explain an empty bottle of Ambien without looking crazy? Why am I in here, and Brett and his chums are off scot-free?* Cecilia could imagine Jody asking, "What's wrong with this picture?" *Oh, Jody, I need you. What have I done?*

A young nurse appearing to be Cecilia's age or younger met them at the door.

"Cecilia Evans?"

"Yep, that's me."

"I'm Tate, and I'll get you checked in. Here's a fancy gown and socks you may have in exchange for all your clothes and shoes," she said while handing her a bag to put her things in.

"Somebody will lock your things up for now. That includes your cell phone and purse."

"My cell phone?"

"Yes."

Too tired to argue, Cecilia dropped it in the bag with her clothes and handed it all over to the nurse.

"Your room is ready. Follow me, Ms. Evans."

"You can call me Cecilia."

Tate turned and smiled. Cecilia suspected there was more to the young blonde nurse with the gentle demeanor than what met the eye.

The blue-gray room with padded walls was sterile and had no decorations. There were no windows to show any parcel of blue skies or sunshine. A distinct hint of disinfectant wafted up Cecilia's nostrils. A small plexiglass insert in the door allowed someone to look in without actually opening the door—her private prison cell.

I guess I'm marked now as an actual suicide prevention case. Well, that's not gonna happen again. Brett, you and your pals will pay if it's the last thing I do. Who needs evidence to get even? Her jaw muscles tightened as she fantasized revenge for what they had done to her.

"This pillow sucks!" she cried as she tossed and turned on the hard mattress, trying to find a position that would prevent her arm from going to sleep. "Sophia, I'll be home soon. I'm sorry I left you like this." Every time she closed her eyes, the memory of Judd's warm embrace soothed her anxious thoughts until Brett entered, ripping her out of his arms and throwing her on the bed. She stared into the darkness, afraid of closing her eyes and seeing them strip off their clothes. Their laughter still rang in her ears. About the time she fell asleep, Tate knocked on the door and came bustling in, full of energy, giving no regard to the sleepless night she had endured.

"How did ya sleep last night?"

"Just fine."

"That's good because you have a busy day, and we adhere closely to the schedule."

Every day's schedule was the same: breakfast, counseling, lunch, group therapy, dinner, bedtime rituals, and lights out.

The questions became monotonous as Cecilia was repeatedly asked the same things as if they didn't believe her. *I'm telling the truth, just not the whole truth. I've said and done all the right things, and I'm ready to go now! Maybe they're keeping me here long enough to see if I'll cave and give them something new to diagnose. Well, that's not gonna happen. I've had years of learning how to bury the truth and convince everyone I'm living the best life. I have a mask for every occasion.*

On the fifth day, Cecilia entered the great room to find tables with easels, acrylic paints, brushes, water jars, and paper towels.

Taking a seat, her eyes became glued to the canvas as she thought of all the hours she had spent painting Sophie into the exquisite garden she hoped would one day be a reality for her beloved angel plant.

"What do you see?"

Cecilia didn't look around. She knew the voice and the familiar smell of his cologne.

"I see a magnificent garden full of flowers singing a sweet melody," she answered.

"Well, you know what to do then. Paint your story, Cecilia."

He walked around the table, stopping by each canvas and giving instructions as people came in and took their seats.

Soft music played in the background as she poured paint onto her palate and began to dip her fingertips in. With all her senses heightened, she moved them across the canvas. Her body began to tingle. She imagined the synapses in her brain firing as her creation came alive. No longer could she hear the background music playing, for her painting was singing its song.

When she looked up, the room was almost empty except for a few stragglers rinsing their brushes and putting paints away.

Where are you, Judd? You're gone, just like that. No goodbyes or excellent job, nothing. I suppose it's better that way.

Cecilia held the canvas close to her nose, and inhaled deeply as if to smell the flowers.

Tate peered over her shoulder. "That's nice."

"Thanks. Does the instructor come here often?"

"He usually comes in once every other week, but he came in extra this week. The patients enjoy his art therapy class."

Cecilia nodded her head as if she understood why.

"Are you ready for dinner?"

"No, I'm not hungry tonight. I'd like to go back to my room."

"Okay, if you get hungry later tonight, the nurse could get you a sandwich."

"Thanks, Tate."

"Hey Cecilia, your artwork is exceptional. You should keep painting."

"I might just do that."

Cecilia lay on her bed and stared at the ceiling. Peace wrapped her up like a warm blanket. "Judd, you came just for me. I know it. Thank you. You gave me what I needed and didn't expect anything in return, just like my *guardian*." Yawning, she closed her eyes and slept all night for the first time since being there.

\

ost in the solitaire game, Cecilia didn't hear Tate come up behind her. "Dr. Turner's looking for you. He'd like to see you in his office."

Cecilia stood up, placed the cards in a neat stack, and ran her fingers through her hair.

"Well, let's not keep the doctor waiting," she said as she followed Tate down the long corridor to his office.

"Dr. Turner," Tate called as she knocked on the door and waited for his response.

"Come in."

"Hello, Cecilia," he said as he stood and took her chart from the nurse. "Have a seat, young lady."

After she had been seated, he sat back down and fumbled through the pages. "You've been with us for almost a week now, and you've made good progress. Do you think you're ready to go home now?"

"Yes, sir, I do."

"And what makes you think that?" he asked.

Startled by his quick response with a question, she fired back her answer.

"Sir, to tell you the truth, this is the wake-up call I needed."

"Really?"

"I went straight from college to law school without any breaks and have been driven to accomplish my goal. The one thing I didn't do is take time to smell the flowers, you might say."

"I see."

"The day I decided to go to sleep, well…"

"You mean, the day you decided to commit suicide."

"Yes, sir, that day. I was tired. I didn't feel I could finish the race. But now I see it's not a race. It's just part of the journey, and I don't have to be the best at everything as long as I do *my* best and allow some time to smell the flowers I was talking about. Sometimes, I guess we have to hit rock bottom to learn that. And that's what happened to me. This will not happen again; I can promise you that."

"And why can you do that now?"

"I have a purpose: to help those who can't fight for themselves. I have spent the last seven years preparing to do just that."

"Sounds pretty impressive, Miss Evans, but how can I be sure you're telling me the truth?"

"You can't, sir. Time will produce the evidence needed to conclude the truth. Thank you all at Oak Ridge for helping me sort things out."

"You're speaking like a true lawyer, Miss Evans. I believe you're ready to leave and continue your journey."

He called for Tate to come back and escort her back to her room.

"Miss Evans, I'm glad we could help you. I'll write orders for your discharge. I do recommend you follow up with counseling as an outpatient."

"Thank you, Dr. Turner."

"Tate, I've written orders for Ms. Evans' discharge. Will you help her back to her room now?"

"Thank you again, Dr. Turner."

"You're welcome."

Cecilia looked back at Dr. Turner, who was busy on his computer, and said, "Goodbye."

And just like that, I'm dismissed. And you, Dr. Turner, never did unravel the truth of this case.

"I'll be right back with your belongings and discharge instructions," Tate said. "Do you have someone who can pick you up, or would you like us to call a cab for you?"

Cecilia thought about Judd but quickly dismissed the idea. *Before I take on anything new, I need to get home and see what I've missed for the last week.*

"Just call me a cab if you don't mind."

It wasn't long before Tate returned with Cecilia's purse and cell phone, and went over the discharge instructions.

"Your cab is by the front entrance. If you're ready, I'll walk you down."

"I'd like you to have this, Tate," Cecilia said while handing her the picture she had painted in art therapy.

"Really?"

"Yes. And thanks for all you do here. I admire the way you're able to keep things light when people come in carrying such heavy burdens. I appreciate that."

Thank you and thanks for this picture. This is a real treasure. I bet you're gonna be famous one day!"

Cecilia smiled and hugged her. "Maybe so."

Downstairs, she hesitated before opening the car door of the yellow cab, and looked back at Tate.

"You can do this, Cecilia."

Smiling, she entered the cab, carrying her purse and secrets...so many secrets.

"1301 Ridgewood Drive, please."

"Yes, ma'am."

Cecilia was glad the cabbie didn't try to strike up any conversation. Her mind was preoccupied with anticipation of opening the front door to her apartment and entering alone.

"Here we are, miss. It'll be twenty dollars."

Cecilia handed him twenty-five and stepped out with her hospital bag, hurrying to get in before any neighbors came out. She wasn't sure who had seen her dramatic exit last week and wasn't in the mood to chit-chat about it.

"Sophie girl, how are you? I'm sorry I left you all alone. You look parched." She took the glass she had used to swallow all the pills from the coffee table and filled it with water. "Here you go, girl. Have a drink. I promise never to leave you again."

42

S ITTING ON THE couch, Cecilia fired up her computer to check for missed assignments. *How am I ever going to face Brett to do that debate? What kind of lawyer will I be when I let this go without seeing them put away for good? I never let on that I was gang raped. My apartment was all clean, and I had taken a shower and put on fresh clothes. I threw all the evidence away. Rape wasn't on their radar at the hospital, so no vaginal exam was done; no evidence was collected. I never mentioned anything about it at Oak Ridge. Would it matter anyway? His dad's a prestigious city lawyer in one of the most prominent law groups in town. He's known as a shark. I'm sure he'd find some way to turn it around on me.*

Scrolling through her messages, she noticed that Jody had called several times and wanted her to call back.

Tomorrow Jody. Not tonight.

Making sure all the doors were locked and the deadbolt was on, Cecilia scooped Sophie up and went to shower. "Soph, as soon as I can, we're moving from this place. We're gonna have a house of our own. Do you hear that, girl? Yeah, you like that? Great! I'll start looking."

Being in my PJs and out of that place feels so good. Cecilia made a grilled cheese sandwich and sat on the couch to eat. She scrolled through her contacts until she found Judd's. Staring at the number, she started to call several times and then laid the phone down on the coffee table.

Judd, did you say you loved me when I was in the hospital, or was I just dreaming?

THE NEXT DAY, Jody called first thing.

Cecilia inhaled deeply and exhaled slowly, trying to relieve the tension in her neck before answering the phone. *I'm not gonna tell her what happened.*

"Cecilia? Are you all right?" Jody asked with great concern in her voice.

"Yes, why?" she answered, wondering if Judd had called her.

"Have you read the paper?"

"What are you talking about?"

"The murder on campus. Brett and three other guys have been charged with raping and murdering a freshman. She was found dead in her dorm room. An autopsy was done, and it looks like she died from a date rape drug. Two students saw Brett and the others coming out of her room the night before she was found. According to the time they were seen leaving and her time of death I don't think they knew she had died, but police found DNA samples matching all of them. They've been arrested with no bail! Brett's dad won't be able to get him out of this one. I can't imagine he'd do something like that. I knew he was a slimeball but never took him as a rapist. Didn't you go out with him when you were working on that debate?"

Cecilia, stunned and feeling faint, tried to answer. "Not really. We just went over questions for our teams to ask for the debate. When did this happen?"

"I think about a week ago, and now it's all over the papers!"

"Jody, may I call you back? I'm not feeling so well."

"Cece, do I need to come there?"

"No, I'll be okay. I need some time to process this news."

"You call me, and I'll jump on a plane and be there in a minute. Do you understand? And if not now, we need to see each other soon. I miss you. I'm worried about you. This whole thing gives me creepy chills."

"I will. We'll talk later."

Cecilia sat on the floor, barely able to breathe. "Oh, God," she cried, "What have I done?" *Maybe I could've saved her if I had said something; maybe she wouldn't be dead. Oh, God. I'm so sorry. How many other girls had they done this to before me? How many were too afraid to talk? Afraid of more trauma by having to relive everything again with no guarantee that justice would be served. She's dead now, and if I had just spoken up... Did Brett bank on the fact that I would be too ashamed to say anything? Did he want to put me in my place? To strip Miss Summa Cum Laude of all honor and pride?* She remembered his evil eyes as he mocked her. In an attempt to escape his voice that tormented her, Cecilia put her hands over her ears.

"I need water." She got up from the floor and made her way to the kitchen. As she poured herself a tall glass, she remembered how she had gotten water to swallow her sleeping pills and started to tremble. "What was I thinking? I tried to kill myself over someone like you, Brett McCain!"

Cecilia went to find her computer to see if Professor Greene had sent an email about the campus murder. "How can we debate the death penalty when one of his students may end up on death row?"

After finding an email from him, Cecilia paused and cleared her throat before preceding to read it. *The debate on capital punishment has been canceled until further notice due to the death of a student on campus.*

Staring at the screen, Cecilia felt heat rising in her face as her body tingled.

*How ironic you oppose the death penalty, Brett, because the state of Texas does **not**,* she thought, still numb to the reality of the news.

C ECILIA FUMBLED THROUGH her discharge papers, looking for the counselor's name that Dr. Turner had recommended.

"You were right, Jody. I need help," she said while calling the number on the page.

"New Hope Christian Counseling Services. Mary speaking. May I help you?"

Christian?

"May I help you?" she repeated.

"Yes, ma'am. I'd like to make an appointment to see a counselor. Dr. Turner treated me last week at Oak Ridge Psychiatric Hospital and recommended your group."

"Let's see. We do have an opening on Friday at 11:45 with Dr. Wall."

"I can do that."

"Great. Bring your insurance card and photo ID when you come."

"Thank you. I will."

Cecilia hung up and looked at Sophie. "Christian." *Jody probably prayed for me when she told me to get help.* "I guess it's now or never, Christian or not. Soph, I'm tired, tired of running."

FRIDAY WASTED NO time arriving in Cecilia's mind as she signed in to New Hope Counseling.

"Cecilia," said a well-dressed woman who appeared to be in her early forties. "I'm Dr. Wall, but you may call me Amy."

Following her into a spacious office, Cecilia sat by the window, her chair facing the door. She noticed the picture frames on her desk, showcasing three young children and a handsome, well-built man with the ideal smile.

*It looks like she **has** the perfect little family!*

Dr. Wall noticed her staring at the pictures. "Cecilia, that's my children and husband. We adopted them after trying to have children for years. They're a handful, but we're thankful they're part of our family."

Cecilia could feel herself wanting to run but remained seated and quiet.

"Tell me a little about yourself, Cecilia. I see you're a law student. Do you attend UT?"

"I do. I'll be graduating next semester. I see *you* graduated from the University of North Carolina," she replied, pointing to her degree on the wall behind her desk.

"I did."

"My best friend, Jody, is attending law school there now."

"How long have you been friends?"

"We met at UT and were roommates for four years of undergrad. We're both from North Carolina. I guess we had to come to Texas to meet."

Dr. Wall smiled.

"Her dad graduated from UNC, and she promised him she'd go to law school there if she could come to UT first."

"You didn't want to return to North Carolina for law school?"

"No. I like it here in Austin." Cecilia felt the sweat build up on her palms as she feared what Dr. Wall might ask next.

"What would you like help with, Cecilia?"

Crossing her arms and shuffling in her chair, Celia responded, "I will lay it out on the table, Dr. Wall. I've tried to fix myself, but I'm too broken to put myself back together again. So much so that I tried to commit suicide a couple of weeks ago after years of living in pain."

Hanging her head down, she began to speak in a near whisper. "My dad sexually abused me until I was about twelve." Swallowing hard, she continued. "At sixteen, I got pregnant by a boy I met at a party and didn't even know. They told me it was just tissue, but I knew better. I still had an abortion. I don't deserve to live, but here I am. I'm so ashamed of my life. I've only told my friend Jody about my abortion. I've never shared my other secrets with anyone else before today. What happened recently was something I didn't feel I could live with. I was..." Cecilia looked down and got quiet. Dr. Wall remained silent.

"I was...I was drugged and raped by someone I know and his buddies." Cecilia looked up at Dr. Wall and began to cry. "There, I said it."

Dr. Wall began to speak in a calming and gentle voice. "Congratulations."

Cecilia looked puzzled.

The doctor continued. "I'm proud of you and your courage to open up to me. Cecilia, you are a strong young woman who took a crucial step today. You told the beginning of your story. I hear you, and I see you."

Cecilia stopped crying and sat up. She certainly had not expected that response from Dr. Wall.

"I'm here to help. Can you tell me what you want me to help you with?"

"I don't believe I'll ever forgive myself for aborting my baby, and I don't see how I'll ever be able to forgive Brett and his buddies or my dad for what they did to me. I feel so much hate in my heart, and I don't like what it's doing to me, but at the same time, I don't want to let go of it."

"How is your spiritual life?"

"My spiritual life?" Cecilia asked, caught off guard. "Oh yeah, I remember, you're a Christian counseling group. Is anyone allowed to come here that doesn't believe in your God?"

"Of course. We're all spiritual beings, though. If you don't mind, I'd like to explore that more with you at some point."

"Alright, I guess so. Jody's a Christian, and she always tried to sneak her religion in on me," she said with a half smile. "She's the one who told me to get professional help when we were in school together."

"Jody must be a good friend."

"She's the best. I did go to church when I was young. My dad made me."

"Did he go with you?"

Cecilia laughed out loud. "No."

"How did that make you feel?"

"Hmm. I guess I'd say confused."

"How so?"

"There was nothing about him that said *church* or *God*. I never understood why he would want me to learn about the good father they taught about when he was not."

"That *is* confusing."

"Yeah, it is. And I have some issues with the *good father* anyway."

"You do?"

"Yes. How could he stand by and let them all do the terrible things they did to me if he was a good father? If he's even real at all?" Cecilia began to tremble and rock back and forth. "I hate them all. I hate them all!" she cried.

"Of course, you hate what they did to you. I hate it, too. Anyone with a right mind would."

Cecilia glanced up to meet Dr. Wall's compassionate glance.

"And do you know who else hates it? God does. God hates it when people use the free will he's given us to use and abuse others."

"Why didn't he stop it? Or prevent it altogether?" Cecilia demanded.

"I can't answer that question, Cecilia. I'm not God. I don't know what he had in mind when he allowed these heinous things to happen to you. But I do know that it grieves him deeply and that he cares. He doesn't stop things from happening altogether, but he does help us heal from the trauma we experience."

"The pain is overwhelming. Unbearable most days. How would I even start to heal?" Cecilia inquired.

"It's a process. We're wounded *in relationship*. Therefore, we are healed *in relationship*. It's just usually a different relationship," Dr. Wall explained. "You may or may not ever get sincere apologies from those who've hurt you, but you can experience empathy and compassion from *someone else,* which can help us heal. I'd like to be that latter person in your life… *if* you feel like you can trust me."

Cecilia paused, her head swimming with disbelief that she could feel such optimism after such a short while. "Well, I guess if you don't have a magic wand with which you can fix me fast, then there's no other way than to wade slowly through the deep with a trustworthy guide. Just tell me what I should do, and as long as you don't try to force the god thing on me, I'll try my best to do it."

Goodbyes were exchanged, and Cecilia left, still digesting her meeting with Dr. Wall.

Sophie, I can't wait to tell you. Something happened in that room today. Dr. Wall didn't try to fix or persuade me to believe in her God. She just listened. She didn't judge me. I felt safe. I wasn't alone anymore with my secrets.

44

FOR WEEKS, CECILIA mulled over her meeting with Dr. Wall before calling Jody. The phone rang several times before she picked up.

"What are you doing this weekend?" Cecilia asked.

"Well, hello to you too!" Jody teased. "Oh, I thought I'd catch the next flight to Texas and aggravate you!"

"Well, that's exactly what I hoped you'd be doing."

Jody didn't speak for several seconds. "Are you all right, Cecilia?"

"I'm not sure. I just need to see you. I want to talk."

"Do you want to *talk* about anything now?"

"No, not on the phone."

"Let me see if I can get a ticket, and I'll let you know. Cecilia, thanks for calling. Hopefully, I'll see you this weekend."

"Thanks, friend. Talk soon," she said, abruptly ending the call.

If I can trust anyone, it's you, Jody.

A FEW DAYS later, Cecilia was at the airport, fidgeting with her clothes in anticipation of Jody's arrival. She paced back and forth by the gate until she saw her big smile. Embracing one another, Cecilia felt a sense of euphoria, and all the tension in her body relaxed for a moment.

"Girl, I've missed you!" Jody said.

"Let's get out of here and get you something to eat. I know you're hungry,"

"How did ya know?"

"Because you're always hungry!"

"Ha ha! Is that Thai restaurant still open?" Jody asked. "We went to it when you first got to campus."

"How about we pick up some Franklin barbecue?" Cecilia asked as her mind wandered to her first meeting with Brett. Going to the restaurant or even close to campus would not be a good idea right now. Even with him in jail, it triggered too many memories.

"Absolutely! Who can say no to Franklin Barbecue? And what was I thinking wearing these heels? Who am I trying to impress anyway?"

"Girl, kick those shoes off. It's boot time! Let's swing by Franklin's and take it back to my apartment. We can eat by the pool if you like. You *did* bring your bathing suit?"

"I did! And my mouth is already watering just thinking about that brisket!"

"I can't wait to see your new place. I bet it's a lot better than our tiny dorm room."

"You have your own room," Cecilia said as she parked the car and helped Jody with her bags.

"This is amazing, Cece!"

"It'll do for now, but I wanna find a house for sale or rent as soon as school is out and I get a job."

"You and me both. I love my mom and dad, but it's not the same living at home after you've been out on your own for a while."

"I couldn't imagine moving back in with my parents." Cecilia got quiet for a moment. "Hey, thanks so much for dropping everything to hop on a plane at the last minute with no questions asked."

"You don't have to thank me. That's what besties do! Now let's change and get to the pool with this barbecue. I'm starving!"

THEY HUNG OUT in the pool, laughing and telling happy stories about the *good old days* until Cecilia's gaze became distant.

Jody reeled her back in when she recited a line from *Casablanca* in Humphrey Bogart's voice and mentioned Judd.

Splashing water on Jody's face, the war was on until Jody yelled, "I surrender!"

Climbing out of the pool, they lay in the warm sun, sunglasses on and hats covering their faces.

"Ya wanna watch *Casablanca* and have some movie popcorn?" Cecilia asked.

"I thought you'd never ask."

Most of the night, they laughed and blurted out their favorite *Casablanca* lines, as they had done when they watched it at the Paramount.

Mid-morning the next day, Jody followed the aroma of fresh coffee to the kitchen.

"Good morning," Cecilia began. "Are you ready for some espresso, bacon, and blueberry pancakes?"

"Let's make that a lot of espresso," Jody suggested, pushing hair from her eyes and marveling at the feast before her.

Cecilia laughed as Jody moaned with every bite. "I always feel like you haven't eaten in weeks."

"You're partly right. I haven't eaten anything *this good in weeks*. I practically live on coffee and bagels."

"I know. Me too. It's no fun to cook for yourself and have no one to hear your moans of appreciation! Is there anything you'd like to do this morning or afternoon?" Cecilia asked. "I know it's been a long time since you've been to Austin."

"I'd like to sit on your couch, drink this fantastic coffee, and hear what's been going on in your life without me," Jody answered.

Cecilia slowly sipped her coffee. "Okay. If that's what you wanna do, that's what we'll do. I did ask you to come so we could talk."

Jody sat on the couch while Cecilia sat Indian-style on the floor.

"I took your advice," Cecilia said.

"What advice was that, Cece?"

"To get professional help."

Jody kept her eyes focused on Cecilia but didn't say anything.

"I'm seeing this counselor named Amy Wall. I told her it was your fault I was there."

Jody didn't laugh or respond.

"She said it might be a good idea to share more of my story with you, including more of my *secrets*."

"I know it was always hard for you, Cece, but I *will* listen."

"You're a great listener but may not want to hear *these* secrets."

"Just keep the espresso coming."

"Well, let me freshen that cup up before I start," she said nervously.

"Mmmm, so good," Jody went on as she wrapped the throw blanket around her legs and made herself comfortable on the couch.

"My dad wasn't a nice person." Cecilia started and then paused for a minute. "He would come into my room when no one was around. I was young." Cecilia took a deep breath and exhaled. "He didn't stop until he realized I might be brave enough to tell someone. But I never got brave enough. That is, until recently, when I told Dr. Wall."

"Oh, Cece, I'm *so* sorry."

"I wasn't sure I would ever heal but thought if I could bury it deep within myself, seal it in a tomb of darkness never to see the light, then perhaps I might just *survive*. There's more." Cecilia began to shake.

Jody moved closer and held her tightly. "Are you sure you want to continue?"

"Yes."

"I'm listening, Cece."

"I went with Brett to dinner to discuss the debate since we were both captains with a group. I didn't know it would upset him, but I mentioned how nice it must be to have your life planned out after he told me how his dad would bring him into his law firm after graduation. He had made several comments about me being Miss Summa Cum Laude. He started drinking more straight whiskey and then tried to shove his tongue down my throat right there at the bar. Later in class, he apologized and said he had an issue with his dad that he was working out. He wanted me to give him another chance. I told him we could continue the debate if he could be civil. Everything seemed to be going okay, so I didn't think anything about it when he wanted the teams to come over to run through a mock debate and have dinner together. I agreed. When I arrived, his friends were drinking and playing poker at the table. He offered me a Coke, which I drank, and before long, my head felt weird. He picked me up and told me that I *was* the party. He kept calling me Miss Summa Cum Laude. He threw me on the bed, and all his buddies took turns raping me. I begged them not to. I wanted to die. Why didn't God let them kill me? It was so terrible. I don't remember anything after that, but I woke up in my bed the next morning with my keys on the counter. Jody, I *tried* to kill myself. I took a whole bottle of sleeping pills, hoping never to wake up. I turned the TV up loud like my dad used to, and the neighbor upstairs called the apartment manager, who then called 911. Judd was there. He saw me like that, Jody. He saw me after I tried to kill myself."

"I'm here, Cece. You're not alone. I'm so sorry for what they did to you."

Cecilia felt all the blood drain from her face as she choked out the words, "Maybe I could have saved her, Jody. Maybe I could've saved the girl on campus if I had pressed charges against them. Instead, I took the coward's way out and tried to kill myself."

"You had no idea what else those monsters were doing, Cece. You were traumatized yourself. Don't take on the death of that girl. For God's sake, they almost took your life."

Cecilia wailed and groaned like she was dying. Years of torment held captive in darkness were released into the light of the atmosphere.

"Oh, God, please help her," Jody prayed. "Help my friend."

"No, Jody, he doesn't help me. He's never been there when I needed him. How can you have faith in a god that let the same thing happen to you?"

"Cece, do you remember when I wanted to leave art therapy class? And then I didn't want to go that Saturday and surprised you by showing up late with my blank canvas? I stood before the class and told them the pictures weren't pretty when I closed my eyes."

"I do."

"Why didn't you ever ask me about that?"

Embarrassed, Cecilia flinched. "I don't know. I guess I was too focused on myself. Maybe I couldn't think of any ugly pictures other than my own. I just clung to the picture I was painting of Sophia. It was the only thing that would bring me peace."

"I'm glad Sophie brings you so much peace."

Cecilia hung her head down and closed her eyes momentarily before reaching for Jody's hand. "Even though we're best friends, we've managed to keep many secrets, haven't we?"

"We have."

"Will you please tell me about the blank canvas?"

"Are you sure?"

"Yes."

"Okay, if I can get through it."

"If you need to stop, it'll be okay."

"I'll try," she said with a shudder. "My dad wasn't like yours, and my heart is broken thinking about what you must have gone through. I grew up in a loving home and accepted Jesus Christ into my heart as a child. I had everything I ever needed or wanted. The night I went to that party, my life changed. Later, when I found out I was pregnant, I went for the abortion alone. I wanted to keep my secret to myself. I was so ashamed and knew it would break my parents' hearts. I saw the ultrasound and my baby's heartbeat, yet I felt the quickest solution would be abortion. That way, my parents wouldn't have to know how I got pregnant. Not long after the abortion, my parents found me in my bed, almost unconscious. I had a very high fever, and they rushed me to the hospital. Turns out I had an infection from the abortion. At the clinic, they had told me there was a minimal risk of infection, but I guess I was the lucky one, or should I say, not so fortunate. The doctor had to give me powerful IV antibiotics for a long time to clear it up. My parents found out I'd had an abortion, but I refused to tell them who the father was. They were so glad I was still alive, they never mentioned it again."

Jody took a long sip of her cold espresso and shifted in her seat.

"Now for the ugly picture," she said, sending Cecilia a long, pained look before she broke eye contact. "The doctors said I'd probably never be able to have children. So, how can I have faith in a god that let the same thing happen to me? To answer your question, Cece, we live in a world full of evil, but this world is not my ultimate home. I have hope because of Jesus Christ. John 3:16 says: 'For this is how God loved the world: He gave his only Son so that everyone who believes in him will not perish but have eternal life.' His Son, Jesus, died a torturous death on the cross to save everyone. He felt every pain we have felt and will ever feel. Yes, He saw what was done to us. It was evil. It was terrible, yet He died on that cross for the men who attacked us, too. Yes, we were both pregnant. And we both know what it's like to be helpless and raped. Yet, we both decided to take the life of our baby. We are no better than a murderer on death row. But Jesus Christ died on that cross to cover the sin of abortion, and when we come to Him and ask forgiveness, He will forgive us and even forget our sin."

Cecilia sat quietly, glued to every word Jody was speaking.

"The reason I left that canvas blank was because I was still grieving the loss of my baby and the thought of never being able to have another one of my own. I can only imagine how God must have felt as He watched his only Son dying on that cross. He loved us so much that He allowed it. His Son paid the price for our sins with His life."

Cecilia reached over to hug Jody as tears streamed down their faces. "I know your final picture was abstract, but what did it mean to you? I never asked you that, either."

"I felt like something beautiful was formed out of chaos and loss. As I painted, my heart became grateful that I could see the beauty. It made my trust in God stronger. Cece, you can trust God. He is always with you. Remember how He sent your guardian angel to watch over you and gave you your angel plant? Won't you give God a try?"

Cecilia looked at Jody but said nothing about her plea to give God a chance. "I'm sorry I was so selfish I didn't even ask about your picture. Maybe I could have helped you more through your pain if I hadn't been so fixated on mine and all my anger."

"You have nothing to be sorry about. You helped by being my friend and going to art therapy with me. I'm so glad you called me to visit and talk. This has been good."

"Thanks, Jody. It's has been good getting these secrets out in the open today. Hopefully, Dr. Wall will help me figure some things out. Maybe, you should talk to someone too?"

"I have been. Being back home triggered lots of emotions and I knew I needed help. It's what I needed, but so was art therapy and being with you. It's all been part of this healing journey."

"I love you, friend."

"Love you, too. Hey Cece, what about Judd? Have you had a chance to talk to him?"

"No, he's pretty frustrated with me. I don't think he'll be calling. The last thing he said when I was in the ER was I had his number. It hadn't changed." She thought of how he had come and set up easels for art therapy at the hospital and how much that had meant to her, yet he hadn't stuck around.

"You could call him."

"I know."

"I hope you do."

45

THE NEXT DAY, Cecilia drove Jody to the airport, where they hugged and said goodbye.

"You could call him," Jody reminded her.

For the next two weeks, Jody's words played in Cecilia's head repeatedly to the point she could concentrate on nothing else. She decided it was the only decent thing to do, even if he refused to talk to her after all the frustration she had caused him. Staring at her cell phone, she called his number.

"This is Judd. I can't take your call right now, but leave your name and number, and I'll get back to you."

"Judd, this is Cecilia. I was wondering if we could talk. Please give me a call if you could make some time to meet. Thanks."

What if he's screening my number and never wants to talk to me again? God, If you're who Jody says you are, would you make something good out of my messed-up life?

It wasn't long before she felt her phone buzzing in her back pocket. It was Judd.

You can do this. You owe him an explanation.

"Hi, Judd. Thanks for calling me back."

"You want to meet?" he asked in a matter-of-fact voice.

"Yes."

"Okay. You're welcome to come over. I'm out in the yard."

"I'd like that. What's your address?"

"1005 Maxey Road."

"I'll be there soon."

Having envisioned how the meeting would go, she drove into his driveway only to find him digging a hole in the flowerbed without a shirt and sweat dripping down his chest.

Taking a small towel from the pocket of his tan denim Carhartt pants, he wiped his face, grabbed the navy V-neck t-shirt from the porch steps, pulled it over his body, and headed to her car.

"Hey, Cecilia."

"Hi. Thanks for seeing me."

"Yeah. I'm glad you called. I'm a little surprised, though. Come on. We can sit on the porch." He sat on the porch swing while she sat on the wicker couch. "Would you like something to drink?"

"Some ice water would be great."

"Coming right up," he said as he went in and returned with her water.

"Thanks," she said, taking a sip. "Judd, I'm not sure where to start, so I guess I'll first thank you for being with me in the ER and showing up at the hospital to do your class. Tate told me it wasn't your normal week to come."

Judd nodded his head.

"The art therapy was the most healing experience I had while in the hospital. The rest of the time, I played a game with the counselors and the doctor by answering their questions with what I felt they wanted to hear so I could just get outta there. I was never truthful with them."

Judd remained quiet, and a moment of silence lingered before she continued.

"When I found out about the murder on campus, I broke and reached out to a therapist. For the first time, I was honest about my past. The poor decisions I had made. The shame and guilt from all my trauma. It was the most freeing experience I've ever had. She congratulated me for being brave enough to share it all with her. Once I spoke the truth, it didn't seem to have the same kind of hold on me. I've got a long way to go, but it was a big step in the right direction."

"Cecilia, I'm glad you were able to get some help. That's good to hear."

"Thanks. I need to ask you to forgive me for all the times I was rude and appeared ungrateful. I kept you at a distance even though I wanted you close because I didn't feel I was worthy of someone kind and loving toward me. I also thought you wouldn't want me if you knew the truth about my past."

"Cece, your past doesn't define who you are. I see a beautiful, smart, kind woman I have loved since the first day she walked into my classroom. Come here," he said as he took her hand and pulled her close. Looking deep into her eyes, he embraced her with both arms. "I love you. Period."

"I'm not sure I can believe that. My past has defined my whole life. How am I supposed to change that? I thought working harder, being the best, becoming successful, and making lots of money would compensate for all the bad and prove I was good enough to be loved. That somehow I could earn love. How can I receive love when I don't love myself? How can I love you if I don't know *how* to love?"

"Let me teach you."

Taking her by the hand, he walked her into the house and into his study, where her prize picture was hanging on the wall beside RJM's abstract.

Cecilia's body tightened, but instead of running, she sobbed. *We decided to take the lives of our babies. We're no better than a murderer on death row,* Jody had said.

Judd pulled her closer to his chest. "I was the anonymous bidder. I would have paid whatever price I had to for your painting because I see you every time I look at it. I bought RJM's painting because you once said you saw hope in it."

"Hey," he said, handing her a tissue, "would you trust me enough to take you to meet the artist that painted this picture?"

"You mean on death row?" she asked, feeling faint all of a sudden.

"Yes."

God, is this part of your plan?

"I guess so," she muttered.

"Trust me, Cece."

"This trust thing is hard, and it's scary."

"I'll be with you. Let me grab my jacket."

Cecilia gazed at RJM's painting, which had once evoked deep anger and hatred. Staring intently, she moved in closer and followed every stroke of the brush with her eyes. There *he* was, hidden in a plethora of colors. An image of a tall, slender man. She ran her hand along the outline of the man's figure. "Could it be? Could it be him? The mysterious guardian?"

God?

Cecilia was so focused on the painting she didn't hear Judd come back into the room.

"Cece, are you okay?" he asked, taking her hand.

"I believe there's a hidden treasure within this piece."

"A treasure? Do you wanna share it with me?"

"I can't. I believe it's a mystery one must unravel for themselves."

Judd stared long and hard at the artwork. "Maybe the treasure is just for you, Cece."

"Maybe so."

THE RIDE TO the prison was long, and Cecilia didn't say much. Her mind was swirling, wondering about the purpose of meeting RJM. All the hatred she had held in her heart didn't seem to be there anymore, yet her stomach felt tied in knots.

Judd looked toward her and again said, "Trust me."

Was he reading my mind?

He parked the car and opened the door for her to get out. Putting his arm through hers, they walked through the revolving door into the prison. Judd emptied the pockets of his Carhartt's, and Cecilia put her purse and belt in a bucket before walking through the scanner. They were escorted to the place where the death row inmates were housed and found the prisoner sitting in a chair. Nothing separated them but a pane of glass. Judd motioned for him to pick up the phone, and he and Cecilia took their seat and did the same thing.

Judd cleared his throat as RJM stared at him. Putting his hand on Cecilia's shoulder, he spoke into the phone.

"Raymond, this is Cecilia."

The shackled young man smiled and said, "It's nice to meet you finally. Judd has told me about you and your beautiful art."

Cecilia didn't speak. She was captivated by his blue eyes and his olive complexion. Something was different about this RJM. He was not what she had imagined a death row inmate to be. He exuded peace. Cecilia shook her head and remained quiet.

"Cecilia, Raymond is the reason I got into art therapy."

She turned away from Raymond to look at Judd.

"How so?"

"Raymond is my half-brother."

"What?" She started to stand but sat back down. She wasn't going to run anymore.

"We had the same mother but different fathers. One night, Raymond and a friend of his robbed a grocery store. When the clerk reached under the counter, Raymond thought he was going for a gun and he shot and killed him. Later that evening, Raymond and a drug dealer were sitting in his car making a deal outside our mother's house. She saw his car and went out to check on him. When she tried to open the door, the drug dealer shot her through the glass. Raymond then shot and killed the drug dealer. When the police came, he was holding our mother in his arms as she died."

A sudden coldness hit her core as she gripped the bottom of her chair with both hands.

"I know this is a lot, but when I saw how you reacted the first time you found out about him, I was afraid to tell you. It took me a long time to forgive him. I hated him." Judd looked up at Raymond and then back at Cecilia. "Raymond came to know Jesus Christ while here in prison. When I had to come and see him, I saw a difference in him and, for some reason, continued to visit him. Here, he introduced me to the One that changed his life. It was here he led me to Jesus Christ. He's the only One that has made it possible for me to forgive. When I found out what Jesus had done for me, I couldn't hold on to the hatred I felt. Raymond and I both know about shame, guilt, and grief. I'm sorry I didn't dare to tell you. I'm sorry I lied to you about who bought your painting. I hope you can forgive me."

Trying to take it all in, she turned her gaze toward Raymond, who sat watching her.

"Cecilia, Judd told me you were intrigued by my art, but when you found out about me, you became very upset and wanted to get rid of it. He said you were angry when my painting was next to yours at the art exhibit. Would you mind if I asked you why?"

Unbelievable. A death row inmate, a murderer, questioning me?

Cecilia sighed. *Why **did** I get so angry? Didn't I do the same thing? Was it me I was furious with?*

Cecilia took a long, deep breath and slowly let it out before she spoke. "I don't think I knew until right now. You see, I am guilty of murder, too. My murder was legal. Since the day I chose to abort my baby, I've been in prison, yet I look free and walk freely. This prison has kept me from loving others because I can't love myself. I can't forgive myself for what I did. When I found out you were guilty of murder, I felt you deserved to die. I didn't believe you should have had the freedom to display your art. Maybe having your painting beside mine reminded me of what I deserved."

His blue eyes pierced her soul. "I do deserve to die, and I probably will be executed, short of a miracle, for what I did. But when that day comes, I will stand before a judge who says I'm not guilty because Jesus paid my debt when he hung on the cross and died for me. He paid the price for my sin so that I can live forever with my heavenly Father. He forgave me, and because of God, I could forgive myself. Even though I wear shackles, I am free because of what He did for me. There's a scripture that says he forgives our sins as far as the East is from the West, and he forgets them for his own sake. He will do the same thing for you if you let Him."

With trembling hands, Cecilia looked to Judd and then back to Raymond. "I want that."

"Then tell him you're sorry for what you did and that you believe he paid the price for you to be free from your prison when he hung on that cross. Invite him to be the Lord of your life, to give you a new life in Him."

Cecilia bowed her head and whispered, "I'm sorry, God, for my abortion and for all the hate I've carried in my heart. Please forgive me. I believe in who You are, and I want to be yours."

She looked up and saw Raymond nodding his head. Judd took her hand and squeezed it firmly.

Cecilia smiled as tears fell down her face.

The guard motioned that Raymond's time was up. Judd took her by the hand as they walked to the revolving door. Cecilia placed her hand on the glass and remembered. This time, she stepped through the door—free.

There, in the distance, standing under the old oak tree, Cecilia saw him—the tall, slender man. It was him—her guardian. She raised her hand to acknowledge him. He tipped his hat, smiled, and went on his way.

Epilogue

Seven years later

ECILIA'S ATTENTION SHIFTED from Mary Bell eating breakfast to Sophia proudly sitting by the window. In the early morning sun, Sophia's velvety leaves shimmered just as they had when Cecilia first saw her in the hospital window sixteen years ago. She could never find another of her kind, so she remained her unique angel plant with beautiful crimson blossoms that bloomed every spring. Over the years, they sometimes transferred her to a more prominent planter or replaced it if it got damaged. Now about as tall as Mary Bell and weighing almost as much, she would find her new home in the special garden Cecilia had dreamed about for years.

Judd had backed the truck to the patio near the dining room french doors. Josh had come over to help him load Sophia into the back of the pickup.

"Daddy, I'm not sure I want Sophia to leave us," Mary Bell said.

"Do you remember when we talked to you about the special garden in town where Sophia would live with the other plants?"

"Yes, the one where mommies and daddies can go to sit and remember their babies that are in heaven."

"That's right. We can visit Sophia, too. We'll have to pull weeds and make sure the garden is cared for so it will always be beautiful."

"I can help with that!"

"Yes, you can. Now you and Mommy better get ready so you can meet us there. Today's the big day. You can help cut the ribbon when we dedicate Sophia's Garden."

Cecilia smiled. "Yep, Gramma and Pops, and Aunt Ana and Uncle Josh and Josh Jr. and Auntie Jody will all be there, so we better get going."

With the doors open, Cecilia paused to hear the waves crashing on the shoreline. Being back on the Outer Banks of North Carolina was like a mosaic where all the broken parts had come together to form a beautiful piece of art. Waking up to the sound of the ocean every day next to Judd, the love of her life, where Mary Bell came in for snuggles and hugs, was more than she could have ever asked for or imagined. Practicing law with Jody, having her family nearby, and today's ribbon cutting for the memorial garden were all a dream come true.

"ARE YOU EXCITED you get to cut the ribbon today?" Cecilia asked.

"I can't wait! Sophia's gonna like her new garden," Mary Bell beamed.

Taking Mary Bell by one hand and carrying her shovel in the other, Cecilia took a deep breath and entered the garden. Judd and those she loved stood behind the ribbon that would soon be cut as she dedicated Sophia's Memorial Garden to all those who had lost babies to abortion, miscarriage, stillbirth, prematurity, or illness.

Judd reached down and proudly helped Mary Bell cut the ribbon as everyone cheered.

Today, Cecilia would dig another hole. A hole big enough for Sophia, her angel plant, where her roots could run deep.

Cecilia put her right foot on the top of the shovel, looked at Judd as he held Mary Bell in his strong arms, and drove the shovel deep into the ground, scooping out the first parcel of dirt.

Looking up, she saw him. The tall, slender man standing in the back of the crowd tipped his hat toward her and smiled.

Her guardian had come.

Cecilia nodded and mouthed the words, "Thank you."

She closed her eyes and tilted her head back to the heavens, feeling the sun kiss her face and a warm wind swirl around her as she heard him say,

I will never leave you. I am with you always…

Discussion Session #1

1. Cecilia was distraught and violently digging holes in her backyard before she passed out in Chapter 1. Have you ever done anything out of character when faced with an overwhelming problem?

2. In Chapter 2, Cecilia had to go out the door to meet her ride to class with a band-aid on her bleeding hand. She was told "not to say anything." Have there been times when you put on an "invisible mask" to cover up the pain or hurt you were carrying inside?

   If so, discuss how that felt and how you handled it.

3. The "angel plant" became very important to Cecilia. What did this gift symbolize to you? Have you received a special gift from someone or held onto something of comfort during a difficult time?

Discussion Session #2

1. Cecilia left for college before resolving issues with her father. She worried about her mother's safety. How do you suppose she felt on her long trip to Austin, Texas? Have you ever had to leave a situation without being able to "fix it" for yourself or others involved?

2. Becoming very angry, Cecilia stormed out of the restaurant after the waitress shared what the scripture tattooed on her arm meant to her in Chapter 14. Look up Deuteronomy 3:16. Have you ever felt forsaken by God or by someone who was supposed to be there for you?

Discussion Session #3

1. Although intrigued by RJM's artwork, Cecilia discovers that he is a criminal on death row convicted of murder and her only thoughts are to trash his painting in Chapter 20. At the art show, she runs away when she finds her painting displayed next to one of his. Have you found there are repetitive triggers in your life that evoke strong emotional reactions? How do you handle these reactions?

2. Judd had only shown Cecilia respect and care, yet she continued to push him away.

   Cecilia didn't feel she deserved to be loved by anyone "good" because of her past.

   Have you noticed patterns like this in your life? If so, what do those patterns look like for you?

3. Judd continued to see the good in Cecilia even when she could not see it in herself.

   Take a moment to think about who has encouraged you along your life's journey.

   Is there someone you know who needs to be encouraged today?

Discussion Session #4

1. Cecilia did not want the law involved, even to the point that Brett and his buddies would go unpunished. Have you ever ignored something instead of dealing with it because it was too painful or embarrassing?

2. After Cecilia is traumatized at Brett's apartment, she loses all hope and tries to commit suicide. Have you ever felt so hopeless you could not see how things would get better? How did you overcome your feelings and move forward? Are you in a place of hopelessness now?

Discussion Session #5

1. Who did you perceive the *guardian* to be? Have you ever felt like someone was watching over you even though you couldn't see them?

2. Cecilia thought she could never forgive herself or others. What effects did unforgiveness have on her life and those around her? Do you have unforgiveness in your heart toward yourself or others? How has that affected you?

If you feel you need help with any of the issues depicted in this book, please reach out to someone! Support is available at the resources below. If you are having suicidal thoughts, **call or text** the suicide prevention hotline and seek help immediately.

Resources

PDI - Pregnancy Decision Line

Call **1-866-281-3029** for free, confidential help.

Crisis Text Line

Text "Brave" to 741-741
Free 24/7 support for anyone in crisis.
Text from anywhere in the United States, anytime, about any type of crisis.
Someone will receive the text and respond from a secure online platform.
This trained volunteer crisis counselor will help you move from a hot moment to a cool moment.

988 Suicide & Crisis Lifeline

Call/Text/Chat 988 or Call 1-800-273-TALK (8255)
Free 24/7 support for anyone experiencing emotional distress or a suicidal crisis.
When people call, text, or chat 988, they will be connected to trained counselors who are
part of the existing Lifeline network. These trained counselors will listen, provide support, and connect them to resources if necessary.
The previous Lifeline phone number (1-800-273-8255) will always remain available to people in emotional distress or suicidal crisis.

National Sexual Assault Hotline

1-800-656-HOPE (4673)

Free, confidential, 24/7 support. Chat option available at rainn.org.

<u>National Human Trafficking Hotline</u>

1 (888) 373-7888
SMS: 233733 (Text "HELP" or "INFO")
24/7 support in English, Spanish, and 200 more languages.
Website: http://humantraffickinghotline.org

Self-Evaluation

Make two columns on a piece of paper.

Title one side: *The worst things I have ever done to anyone.*

Title the second side: *The worst things anyone has ever done to me.*

Do you believe God has forgiven you? If you answered yes, are you willing to forgive those that have hurt you?

Review the second column and ask God to show you any unforgiveness in your heart toward those who have hurt you.

This is a forgiveness prayer that I have used many times.

Lord, I forgive

LORD, I GIVE You permission to take the judgment and the bitterness out of my life. I do not want this in my life. I surrender it to You and ask You to remove it, heal me where I have been wounded, and forgive me where I have sinned. I choose not to blame or hold the actions of others against them. I hereby surrender my right to be paid back for my loss by the one who has wounded me or who has sinned against me. In so doing, I declare my trust in God alone, as the Righteous Judge.

Father God, bless them in every way.

In Jesus' name, AMEN.

Christ died on the cross so that we could be forgiven and reconciled to God. I choose to forgive others because He has forgiven me.

If you have never accepted Jesus Christ as your Lord and Savior and want to now, say this prayer with me.

Lord Jesus, I have sinned against You and I am sorry. I choose to turn away from my sins and ask You to forgive me. I believe You are the Son of God. I believe that You came to earth and died on the cross for my sins. I believe You rose from the dead three days later. I ask You to come into my heart and fill me with Your Holy Spirit. I accept and confess You as my personal Lord and Savior. Thank You for saving me.

If you have said this prayer, tell someone the good news of what He has done for you! I would love to hear from you also. I encourage you to find a Bible-believing church where you can grow in Him. You may email me at **donnamcelroyLLC@gmail.com.**

There is therefore now no condemnation to those who are in Christ Jesus, who do not walk according to the flesh, but according to the Spirit. Romans 8:1 NKJV

About the Author

DONNA MCELROY IS an author, artist, board-certified mental health coach, and registered nurse. Her passion is to minister to women about the truth of God's love so that trauma from their past doesn't rob their future. She speaks to women about how the transforming love of God turned the broken pieces of her life into a beautiful masterpiece. Donna has volunteered at pregnancy testing centers to offer hope and practical assistance in navigating  unplanned pregnancies. She has also worked in the newborn nursery, as a special care nurse in the NICU, and as a lactation consultant for twenty-one years. Donna graduated from the B.L.A.S.T. (Building Leaders, Authors, Speakers, and Teachers) mentoring program with Shannon Ethridge and has been a part of a B.L.A.S.T. tribe for two years.

Donna and her husband, Mark, live in southeastern Pennsylvania, where she leads a local Kingdom Writers Association chapter to provide a community for Christian writers to support one another in their calling. They love bike riding, watching fireworks, and spending time with their adult children and grandchildren on the Outer Banks of North Carolina.

Contact Donna via email at donnamcelroyLLC@gmail.com
Instagram: Shulamite1
Facebook: Donna McElroy
Website: DonnaMcElroyLLC.com

Quill and
Heart Publishing

Made in the USA
Middletown, DE
07 December 2025

22373019R00145